Becoming Fools

Ryan Zak

Written in 2009
Published by ZakBooks in 2018

BOOKS BY RYAN ZAK
(also writes as A.J. Santiago and Cadmius Roper)

Novels
Becoming Fools

Travel
Peace Found Me (Memoirs of Mexico Pt I)
Into the Light (Memoirs of Mexico Pt II)

Children's and Picture Books
The Heartbeat Purpose
Jeff
David's Busy Day
James and the Giant Beard

Short Stories
Hazel
Jesus in Las Vegas

From *Becoming Fools*

"If only I could get my hands on a bottle of
Vivacious Vincenzo's Special Shampoo Formula
For Men, I could die a happy man."

~

"The worst thing for monkeys would be if we
started treating them like humans."

~

"There is a point to all this. I'm sure of it."

~

"I want to preserve your heart in a jar
and throw it to the bottom of the ocean,
so that when humanity fails in a million years,
they'll have a shining example of where to begin
again."

~

"It seems so simple. Our only job is to be kind."

~

"If I should ever die,
The last words from my lips
Will be "Thank you to whomever
Created all of this."
And if I should live forever,
I'll utter those same words,
But I'll sing them every day
To the trees and to the birds."

~

"Death is a dream,
With music and dancing trees.
If you wish to turn it off and just sleep,
You can do that too."

Letter to a Literary Agent, 2010

To whom it may concern,

First, thank you for taking the time to look at the debut novel of an unpublished young author.

Becoming Fools took me two years to write. It has been edited and rewritten twice. It totals 135 pages, 33 chapters, 50,038 words.

I would describe *Becoming Fools* as philosophical fiction, along the lines of the novels of Kurt Vonnegut. It is absurd, thoughtful, silly, sometimes bleak, but ultimately hopeful.

The initial idea for this novel was inspired by Rule #3 from Kurt Vonnegut's 8 Rules for Writing: "Every character should want something, even if it is only a glass of water." So I set out to write a novel involving characters who all *want* seemingly insignificant things, but who follow their trivial desires to the very end with all their hearts.

Though I have been writing regularly for many years, I realize that my style is not yet fully developed- this process will likely take the remainder of my life- and as such, I am open to editing and revamping this novel if someone with more knowledge and experience recommends it.

Thanks again for your consideration.

Sincerely,

- Ryan Zak,

Author Introduction, January 2017

This is my first finished novel. I wrote it when I was 21.

The words came to me in jolts of inspiration, connections were unconsciously formed, and the story largely wrote itself. My main task was to get it all down on paper before it disappeared.

It lacks many aspects that supposedly make for a good book.

While it contains certain temporal inspirations and points of focus, it also hints at the larger ideas and areas of contemplation- human potential, purpose, nonsense, wonder, kindness and understanding- that will likely live on and re-appear in different forms in my future writings.

I choose to publish it because it represents an honest effort to express something I had within me to express at the time.

I hope you enjoy my first finished novel. It will only get better from here.

Sincerely,

- Ryan,

Nothing happens for a reason, but everything can easily be assigned one.

Birds fly because they have wings.
Fish swim because they have fins.
Humans die because we are mortal and alive.

The events in this book did not happen for a reason. But I will do my best to explain along the way.

INTRODUCTION

I'd like to introduce you to some people:

Arthur

Arthur is in fifth grade.

His favourite thing to do is breathe through his nose.

Arthur can stay entertained for hours relaxing against a wall, feeling the air as it tickles the tiny hairs inside his nostrils:

In. Out. In. Out.

Sometimes he switches it up:

In. In. Out. Out.

Or if he's feeling adventurous:

In! In! In! Oouuut.

When the air tickles Arthur's nose hairs too much it makes him sneeze. Arthur has a fear of sneezing.

Dr. Fern couldn't find the medical term for Arthur's condition, so he made one up: Dr. Fern told Arthur that he had "Achoophobia" (see appendix).

Arthur always sneezes five times, which is odd because sneezes usually occur in pairs.

This is all very important.

Arthur believes that sneezing can cause complete memory loss. When Arthur was 10 years old he read a children's book in which the main character sneezed quite violently and wiped out his memory. It was a work of fiction. But nobody told Arthur.

If a sneeze ever snuck up on Arthur and shot out of his face, he would fall into a panic and immediately yell out the 66 books of the Bible.

Arthur had memorized the 66 books of the Bible when he was 8 years old.

Because Arthur was always sneezing and yelling out the books of the Bible, his school teachers suspected that he might be mentally handicapped.

In grade 3 Arthur won the spelling bee and scored the highest mark on the IQ test. After that, Arthur's teachers weren't sure if he was smart or dumb.

"Aaaachhoooo! Genesis Exodus Leviticus Numbers Deuteronomy..."

Karl

Karl is Arthur's younger brother. He is in third grade.

Karl was originally supposed to be named Earl, after his mother's favourite flavor of tea, but the nurse at the hospital made a spelling mistake on his birth certificate.

There is not a flavor of tea with the word *Karl* in it. But if there was a flavor of tea with the word *Karl* in it, "Karl Tea" perhaps, I don't think anyone would drink it. It doesn't sound very appealing.

Karl Tea.

Karl doesn't have many friends. He might even have no friends at all. Nobody knows for sure.

Jim

Jim is Karl and Arthur's father. Jim isn't named after anyone famous.

Jim is almost entirely bald, yet he still shampoos twice a day. If you ask him why, he'll tell you that he likes how it makes his head smell.

The company Jim works for, Happy Steel Co., recently decided to go on strike.

Jim's favorite food is brownies.

This is all very important.

Sheila

Sheila is Karl and Arthur's mother and Jim's wife.

Sheila never uses profanity in the presence of her family. If Sheila stubs her toe, all she'll say is, "Wang, dang, dang!"

Lately, Sheila has been sleeping with her head at the bottom of the bed and her feet at the top, next to Jim's head. If you ask her why, she'll tell you that Jim's breath reeks of stale chocolate.

Oh yes, I almost forgot. Sheila is hiding an enormous secret from her family.

CHAPTER 1

"This too is meaningless" – King Solomon

****

Sheila leaned over the counter, methodically spreading peanut butter onto a row of open-faced whole-wheat bread. She slapped the pieces together, working her way down the row like an assembly line. Her hands moved with machine-like precision as she sliced the sandwiches diagonally in half and dropped them into three brown paper bags labeled, "Jim," "Arthur," and "Karl."

Jim sat at the round wooden kitchen table stirring a dark brown powder into a tall glass of milk. The gentle morning sunlight shone through the small square windows at the rear of the kitchen, illuminating Jim's balding head like a phosphorescent bowling ball. Jim groaned with pleasure as he took a sip of his chocolate drink. It tasted like magic.

Across the table from Jim sat his eldest son, Arthur, who was staring absent-mindedly down into his half-eaten bowl of cereal. Arthur's glass of orange juice was a dark shade of yellow, and not orange as the name would have you believe. The spoon Arthur had been using to eat his cereal now rested on the floor beneath his chair. Four minutes had passed since it had fallen out of his hand and clattered noisily to the kitchen tiles. The glare from Jim's head reflected into Arthur's eyes. Arthur's eyelids fluttered. His narrow nostrils flared as he took a deep breath. Arthur smiled, then frowned, then smiled once more, switching from dream to reality and back again. Arthur dreaded Monday mornings. He also dreaded waking up early. He also dreaded being in fifth grade. But most of all, Arthur dreaded being unpopular.

****

Sheila opened the fridge and took out three cherry-flavored juiceboxes. "Karl," she yelled towards the living room. "Karl, you have to leave for school in five minutes." Her voice was low-pitched and scraggily, like a tired poodle. Sheila straightened up and banged the back of her head on the edge of the freezer door. "Wang, dang, dang!" she yelled.

Sheila's exclamation roused Arthur from his sleepy trance. His head fell forward and his nose dipped into his cereal bowl. Shocked by the cool milk, he jerked backwards, fell awkwardly from his chair and sprawled onto the floor. Through sleepy, slatted eyes, he saw the spoon lying under his chair, and laughed. "What's a spoon doing under my chair?"

Jim's eyes widened. He shot up from his chair and his hip knocked against the table, causing his half-filled glass to tip over. Thick brown liquid came streaming out and seeped off the edge of the table onto Arthur's face. Jim thought that Arthur had said, "Why don't you wash your hair?" and not "What's a spoon doing under my chair?" Jim disappeared in the direction of the bathroom. "Thanks for the reminder son!" he called back to Arthur.

Arthur didn't hear his father. He had brown milky liquid in his ears.

****

Karl sat cross-legged on the shaggy orange carpet, staring tiredly up at the television. On the screen was the extremely old face of Ronnie Frumpton, lead anchor of the *Turtle Pond Morning News Program*. Ronnie Frumpton was introducing the live interview portion of the show. Following the live interview would be the weather report, which often served as the sad climax of the morning.

Ronnie Frumpton stopped mumbling and scratched his armpit, signaling to the producer that he was finished speaking.

The screen cut to a shot of the main street of Turtle Pond, Turtle Pond Road, where amateur reporter, Bull Whalelike, was lumbering down the street towards an unidentified man. Bull Whalelike's enormous girth shook with each step as he struggled to catch up to his target. Karl was reminded of a 300-pound astronaut attempting to sprint on the moon.

"Excuse me! Sir!" Bull Whalelike caught up with the man he was apprehending. The man stopped walking and turned to face Bull. The man was wearing a long brown jacket with the collar pulled up around his face. He waited patiently as Bull put his hands on his knees and wheezed, completely out of breath. As the camera zoomed in on the man's face, Karl gasped in excitement. The man was Reynold Reynoldson, the most famous person in Turtle Pond, and the only true celebrity to ever emerge from within the town's borders.

Indeed, Reynold Reynoldson's slender face was plastered all over Turtle Pond. His portrait hung proudly in the front hall of Turtle Pond Public School. His face was painted on the front window of Luigi's Italian Barbershop. A bronzed statue of his muscular figure stood on the lawn in front of Town Hall. An outside visitor might easily believe that Reynold Reynoldson was some sort of mythical being, worshiped and revered by the entire town. This was not far from the truth.

Reynold had won the admiration of the people of Turtle Pond three-and-a-half years ago when he miraculously set two World Records in the same day. First, Reynold set the World Record for creating the world's largest rubber band ball. Then, three hours later, in a stroke of genius, Reynold Reynoldson set the second record for jumping over the world's largest rubber band ball on a motorcycle.

Reynold Reynoldson faced the fat reporter

with an expression of disinterest and embarrassment.

Bull Whalelike struggled to stand upright. "Hi Reynold," he said breathlessly. "I'd like to ask you a couple questions for *Turtle Pond Morning News.*"

Reynold shuffled his feet uncomfortably and nodded.

"Reynold," Bull wheezed. "As you are probably aware, there are some pretty nasty rumours spreading around town about you."

Reynold's nod was almost imperceptible.

A hungry glint flashed across Bull Whalelike's chubby eyes. "The question on everyone's mind right now is... *are you a permanium?*" (see appendix). Bull thrust the microphone into Reynold's face.

Reynold stood with his hands shoved deep into the pockets of his long brown jacket. He blinked once and spoke quietly into the microphone. "Yes," he said. "I am."

Bull Whalelike's body shook with ecstasy. It was a disturbing sight to behold. "Oh my God!" said Bull. "Reynold Reynoldson is a permanium! Oh my God!" Bull yelled directly into Reynold Reynoldson's ear.

Reynold blinked once, turned, and walked away down the sidewalk.

Bull Whalelike stared into the camera and flashed a wicked, self-satisfied smile. Little bits of spittle glistened like icing in the corners of his mouth. "Citizens of Turtle Pond," said Bull. "You heard it here first. Reynold Reynoldson is a *permanium!*" He stood proudly and tried to suck in his enormous, unavoidable gut. "This is Bull Whalelike, for *Turtle Pond Morning News*, signing off."

The screen cut back to Ronnie Frumpton, who seemed to have grown older over the course of the interview. "Great story Bull. In other news..."

Karl was no longer listening. His mind was spinning, repeating one burning question over and over: *What* is a permanium?

CHAPTER 2

"We are here on earth to fart around. Don't let anybody tell you any different" – *Kurt Vonnegut*

****

Arthur lagged behind Karl, dragging his feet like blunt rakes over loose stones and dusty gravel. It was a short walk to Turtle Pond School, which sat on Turtle Pond Road, directly in the center of town. To get to school Arthur and Karl had to walk past Turtle Pond Drug Store, Turtle Pond Grocery, Turtle Pond Hardware, and Luigi's Italian Barber Shop. When they reached school they could, if they wanted to, turn around and see their mother taking out the garbage on their front lawn.

****

Turtle Pond was big enough to have its own

school, grocery store and library but small enough so that everybody in town knew everybody else's name. And if somebody so much as farted too loud, the whole town knew about it by the time the rooster crowed.

****

There are 47 roosters in Turtle Pond.

****

I suppose a short history of Turtle Pond is in order... The history of Turtle Pond is more controversial than you know. In his book, *Turtle Pond: A Definitive History*, author Randy McQueen Jr. elegantly describes how the town of Turtle Pond came to be. It's generally agreed that Randy McQueen Jr.'s account is the only true and unbiased record of Turtle Pond's history. The following information is paraphrased from the pages of McQueen's book:

The first settlers in Turtle Pond were a nomadic family of turtle shell traders who had grown tired of being nomads. The family consisted of father, Gerald McQueen, mother, Cheryl McQueen, and fifteen sons whose names I shall omit due to space and time constraints (see appendix). It is said that Gerald and Cheryl McQueen chose to reproduce so ferociously because they needed help harvesting turtles. The turtle shell business was quite taxing, both physically and mentally, and was not a particularly lucrative operation at the time. It required hours of tireless searching, swimming, and chasing, and returned very modest results for a full day's work. Between the two of them, Gerald and Cheryl could catch one sack of turtles a day, sometimes less. As you may or may not know, one sack of turtles does not bring in very much money at the market.

So the McQueens hatched a brilliant business plan: give birth to as many children as possible, and fast! Cheryl's ovaries did not have long before retirement. And so they gave birth to child after child, coincidentally all boys, and the hard labour of catching turtles was outsourced to the little runts as soon as they were old enough to walk. Gerald and Cheryl sat back and watched their business grow.

The McQueen boys soon grew up into strapping young turtle-catching men. They took wives and began to have children of their own. They built homes and raised families. They believed in hard work. They had big hearts and strong bones. Their mantra was this: "More eyes to search, more hands to grab, more turtles in the sack."

****

Years passed. More houses were built and more children were born. The turtle-shell business grew into a booming industry consisting of four generations of McQueens, over 100 employees in all. Gerald and Cheryl McQueen had become the godparents of a massive clan of turtle-catchers. The community rose together each morning and trekked out to the ponds and swamps to catch the unsuspecting, sleepy-eyed turtles while they still slept. It is a little known fact that turtles, when wide awake, can be extremely crafty escape artists.

But this peaceful daily routine would not continue forever undisturbed. Yes, all traditions must come to an end. All great and noble societies must eventually change or crumble to the ground.

This is how Turtle Pond's turtle shell dynasty came to an end: In the year 1908, an undefined, unknown speck of life was born. Upon its entry into the universe, the undefined speck was immediately categorized as a female and named Mary Lou McQueen. She was the daughter of Terrence and Honey McQueen, great-granddaughter of Gerald and Cheryl McQueen, youngest of twelve children, nine brothers and two sisters. Mary Lou grew up an average McQueen girl in every way except one: Mary Lou felt sorry for the turtles. She didn't like catching them and she especially didn't like killing them. She was the first McQueen to ever feel sympathy for turtles.

One morning, Mary Lou decided to stay behind while the rest of her family went out to the ponds. She hid in a cupboard and waited until her family had all left the house. Mary Lou then emerged from the cupboard to find the house completely still and silent. She had never been alone before. All her life she'd been surrounded by McQueens. She didn't know what to do. She liked the feeling. She smiled.

****

Mary Lou's family returned home that evening to find her sitting on the floor with a small turtle in her lap. Her parents were horrified. Turtles were meant to be eaten and harvested for their meat and shells, and nothing more. Turtles did not have feelings. Turtles were not pets. Turtles were dumb animals put on earth for the benefit of humans. Mary Lou's parents took away her turtle and gave Mary Lou a sound scolding in front of her siblings.

The following morning, Mary Lou's youngest brother Dylan joined her in refusing to go catch turtles with the rest of the family. Their parents were helpless. They talked it over and concluded that they could not force their children to catch turtles if they did not want to. So off they went to work, leaving Mary Lou and Dylan behind.

The morning after that, two more siblings joined the revolt and refused to go to work. It went on like this for many days, with the number of McQueens opting out of turtle-catching increasing every day. Two weeks later, almost all of the young McQueens were staying in the village while the older McQueens trudged out to the ponds and swamps.

Those who stayed home found countless ways to entertain themselves. Many of the younger children started keeping pet turtles, which they dressed up in frilly clothing and decorated with crude costumes made of leaves, twigs and berries. They held races between their pet turtles in which the slowest turtle was declared the winner since it was determined to be closest to attaining the desirable nature of an ideal turtle.

Mary Lou kept her very own pet turtle that she named Mr. Waddles. She would dress Mr.

Waddles up and tell him all about how horrible and cruel human beings could be, about how he would probably be a cold, lifeless shell on the wall if the humans had their way. She loved Mr. Waddles more than anything. Mr. Waddles never hurt her, never bullied her, and never stole her belongings, though sometimes she wished he would talk just a little bit more. Even a simple smile or nod would suffice. She had grown a little bit angry with Mr. Waddles when she told him about the horrors of turtle-catching and he had remained silent and expressionless. He hadn't shaken his head or retreated into his shell. He just sat there, completely unaffected. But he was forgiven. Mary Lou didn't hold grudges, not against animals as cute and innocent as a turtle.

****

Tensions between children and parents grew, and the number of turtles caught decreased drastically. Things continued on this way until the community could no longer support itself on turtle's alone. Families were forced to adapt, to diversify and begin their own businesses. One family began to cure smoked meat. Another opened a bakery in their kitchen. Another fashioned all sorts of tools out of stone and wood. This newfound industrialism attracted outside visitors, and many people who came to do business in Turtle Pond ended up staying there and living among the McQueens for good.

This period of revolutionary change is often referred to as, "The Great Turtle Shell Crisis of 1921."

****

And so on.

****

You remember how earlier I said that everybody in town knew everybody else's name? Well Karl was the exception to that rule. Nobody knew who Karl was. In grade two Karl had been introduced to his class as "the new kid in town" on five separate occasions. And every time, the class had clapped half-heartedly for the new kid as he sat down at the same old rusty desk in the back corner.

****

You want more proof? Three weeks ago, Karl accidentally bumped into his Aunt Wendy on the sidewalk, causing her to spill her groceries. Karl bent over to help his Aunt pick up the fallen food and she looked up at him without a hint of recognition and said, "Oh, it's okay kid. You've caused enough trouble already."

****

Last year, the walls of Karl's grade two classroom were painted with giant rainbows and adorned with all sorts of colorful student artwork. This year, however, the walls of Karl's grade three classroom were painted solid, monotone white. There were no decorations. Just plain white walls on all sides. The white walls had been specifically designed by Karl's teacher, Mr. Matthews, a failed philosophy major turned grade three teacher. To Mr. Matthews, the blank white walls represented freedom of thought.

****

Here is Karl's Christmas wish list from last year: "10 tie-dyed shirts"

****

Karl sat in the back corner of the class next to a chubby boy named Willy Kroner. Willy constantly played video games on a hand-held console while leaning back on the rear legs of his chair. Karl had never seen Willy make eye contact with another human being. One time, Willy leaned back too far and tipped over in his chair, banging his head off the radiator with a resounding clang. Instead of crying or picking himself up off the floor, Willy simply lay there on the dirty floor and continued playing his game.

****

Karl had already written his Christmas list for this year. Here is what it read: "10 white t-shirts"

CHAPTER 3

"We are all geniuses up to the age of ten."
– *Aldous Huxley*

****

The scent of freshly cut grass wafted in through the open classroom window. Arthur closed his eyes and breathed in deeply. His nose made a high-pitched whistling sound, like a snoring baby bird. He smiled and filled his lungs with as much dry grassy air as possible.

In. Out. In. Out.

In. In. Oouuuut.

In! In! In! Ooouuuuuuuut.

This is what Arthur was doing when his teacher, Mrs. Harrison, stormed through the door and slammed her briefcase down on the oversized wooden desk at the front of the room. It made a loud banging noise, like a muted gunshot or a tall man banging his forehead on a low doorframe. Mrs. Harrison performed this strange strutting, briefcase-banging ritual every morning to wake up any students who might still be half-asleep.

"Good morning children," said Mrs. Harrison.

"Good morning Mrs. Harrison," the students mumbled.

Mrs. Harrison's thin smile vanished. "I said,

good morning children." She glared at her students like an angry hawk.

"Good morning Mrs. Harrison," the students mumbled, slightly louder.

Mrs. Harrison let out a sharp breath and massaged the bulging blue vein that ran vertically from her hairline to her nose, separating the left hemisphere of her forehead from the right. As her fingers traced small circles on her brow, she contemplated how she could punish this ragtag group of complacent children. She had just arrived at work and already her day was ruined. Why won't children just behave?

****

There is something you should know about Mrs. Harrison. Though no one had ever said anything to her, or hinted at it in any way, Mrs. Harrison had always suspected that she was a smelly person. Much like when a person chooses not to tell you that there is a piece of lettuce stuck in your teeth, or when a grandchild chooses not to inform their grandmother that she has a full-grown beard, Mrs. Harrison believed that everybody around her could smell her stench but simply chose not to say anything. Because of this, Mrs. Harrison lived her life in perpetual fear, always suspicious that the people around her were thinking horrible things about her. She was intensely paranoid about her odor, even though she had no proof it even existed.

Mrs. Harrison had paid a visit to Dr. Fern and he had invented a new term to diagnose and classify her disorder. Dr. Fern informed Mrs. Harrison that she had "autodysomophobia", or "the fear of smelling terrible" (see appendix).

****

Everyone in the world has a small degree of autodysomophobia. Everyone in the world also has a small degree of "autostultophobia." That is, everyone is afraid they might unknowingly be stupid. God knows your mother wouldn't tell you if you were.

****

Maybe that's what makes people smell bad: all the fear.

****

Usually something terrible has happened to the protagonist by this point in the story. A tragic event has occurred that will probably take the rest of the remaining pages to resolve. Have faith! Perhaps Arthur and Karl will return home after school to find their house burned to the ground and their parents' bones scattered about the lawn. Perhaps Jim will find out that Sheila has been cheating on him with the milkman and will perform an impromptu murder-suicide in a fit of blind rage. I shudder to think of the emotional damage that such an event would incur on young Karl and Arthur. What a wonderful story that would be.

****

Back at Turtle Pond Elementary School, Mr. Matthews was pacing back and forth in front of Karl's class. "You see," Mr. Matthews was saying, "the concepts of 'inside' and 'outside' are fundamentally flawed. When you're *outside* on the playground, you are actually *inside* the world, and when you're *inside* this enclosed, stifling classroom, you are actually *outside* the world." He paused to let his grade three students absorb what he had said.

"And consider the concepts of *indoors* and *outdoors*," he continued, "which don't make any sense at all. Everybody knows you have to go *through* a door to get anywhere. Therefore," he nodded in conclusion, "everywhere is *throughdoors*." He smiled at his students. "It's all a matter of perspective," he said.

Mr. Matthews searched the young faces for any signs of agreement or understanding. Jacob Resnick had fallen asleep in the front row. A thin trickle of spit hung from the corner of his mouth. Mary Kibblet picked her nose and wiped it on the back of Trevor Newsom's shirt. Mr. Matthews may as well have been talking to a classroom full of salamanders.

He frowned and shook his head. His expression lifted slightly as his eyes fell on Karl sitting in the back corner, gazing absent-mindedly out the window. Mr. Matthews studied Karl for a moment, shook his head once more, and slumped dejectedly into his chair.

****

Not a whole lot was known about Mr. Matthews. Here is the extent of popular knowledge about the man: Mr. Matthews lived alone, without any family or friends, save for his orange tabby cat Garfield and his shaggy sheepdog Oscar. He was a very private man and was only seen leaving his house if he was going to school or if Garfield or Oscar ran out of food.

As a young man Mr. Matthews had wanted to become a full-time "philosopher", but had settled for being an elementary school teacher when he learned that nobody would pay him to sit around and think all day.

Mr. Matthews enjoyed being a teacher. He had lots of time to sit around and think, every evening and all summer to be exact, and sometimes during class. Every so often, when Mr. Matthews came up with a particularly delightful idea, he would show up to class in the morning positively bursting with excitement, thrilled to have a human audience with which to share his idea.

The students could always tell when Mr. Matthews had a breakthrough idea to share because he would arrive at school with wild hair and puffy, bloodshot, sparkling eyes. Immediately after sharing his idea with the class he would often fall asleep on top of his desk.

****

On the first day of school, Mr. Matthews had entered the classroom, walked directly to his desk, sat down in his chair and placed his head in his hands. Not knowing what to do, his grade three students sat in silence. After ten minutes passed like this, Mr. Matthews lifted his head and said, "A wise man thinks about death, but a fool just wants to have a good time."

****

After Mr. Matthews had broken the silence on the first day of class, he had handed out a short quiz. It was one of those quizzes that teachers give to their students upon returning to school after a long summer of sweet freedom. These quizzes usually ask questions like, "What did you do this summer?" and "What do you hope to learn this coming year?" The quiz that Mr. Matthews handed out had asked, among other mind-numbing, insulting questions, "What do you want to be when you grow up?"

Karl, attempting to answer as honestly as possible, had written that he wanted to move to Africa to help poor people. When Karl received his quiz back, he found that Mr. Matthews had scrawled a messy, hand-written message on the back. Here is what it read: "Karl, please do not abstain from North America to live an altruistic life of helping people. It's incredibly unfulfilling and will only serve to make you bitter. This phase of compulsive-compassion orientation will soon pass, and when it does, you'll be glad you positioned yourself inside a BMW."

****

Two weeks later, Mr. Matthews was teaching Karl's class about ancient civilizations- pyramids, weapons, torture, pottery, and other beautiful things. In the middle of the lesson, Mr. Matthews suddenly stopped speaking. He studied his 8 and 9-year-old audience with thoughtful eyes.

"You know," he said, "there's a difference between progress and convenience." He held up his cell phone so the class could see it. "All this technology makes our lives faster and more widespread. It saves us time and energy, so we say it is *convenient*. But think about this: a man who lives in a garbage dump can say he lives *conveniently* close to a garbage dump." Mr. Matthews' students exchanged confused glances.

"Technology saves us time and energy, but with what consequences? What are the byproducts? Complacency, laziness, ignorance, dependency, a privileged and oblivious existence." He shook his head as if emptying it of excess weight. "I think of the hunter-gatherer societies of thousands of years ago as the pinnacle of human progress. They lived outside with an extended family and survived by their own hands and wits." He studied his cell phone with disgust, as though looking at a dead animal or a handful of sewage. He threw it down onto his desk, where it shattered into small pieces of plastic.

"Make some tools, find a nice woman, grow some crops, kill an animal, and then relax in a field under the sun. No stress, no cancer, no cars, no pollution. What happy people they must have been." Mr. Matthews' eyes drifted off into space.

****

The school day was almost over. The students' mouths were watering with anticipation of the deep blue sky and crisp, fresh air awaiting them just beyond the white walls. To Mr. Matthews it felt like a perfectly normal day. But what he didn't know was that he was about to say something that would change one of his students' lives forever. That student was Karl.

****

Teaching is a dangerous job. A teacher never knows who's listening.

****

Fun fact: The term "humanitarian" was first used by a physician in 1789 who proposed that capital punishment be carried out by beheading quickly and cleanly on a machine, for humanitarian and efficiency purposes.

That's good to know.

CHAPTER 4

"Most people can't understand how others can blow their noses differently than they do."
– *Ivan Turgenev*

****

At the start of each school day, Mrs. Harrison's students read silently for fifteen minutes. Talking was strictly prohibited. If the book you were reading was funny, you were not to laugh. If it was tragic, you were to keep your tears inside. If it was life-changing, you were to tell no one about it.

Mrs. Harrison's penetrating eyes flitted from one student's face to the next. Upon finding no evidence of tomfoolery or shenanigans, and feeling somewhat satisfied with the wonderfully obedient silence, Mrs. Harrison allowed the corners of her lips to curve slightly upwards.

Then her eyes fell upon Arthur. Her eyebrows slanted inwards, doing their best impression of a pair of dormant pinball flippers. It appeared that Arthur had no interest in silent reading or obeying the rules. Instead of reading silently, Arthur was smiling dreamily and staring down at his nose. His eyes were crossed in the most extreme manner and his nostrils were fluttering in the silent atmosphere. Mrs. Harrison was appalled. She could feel a veiny bulge beginning to form on her forehead. Her vision blurred as she watched Arthur's delicate nostrils expand and contract, changing speeds, whistling a gentle song. Mrs. Harrison could feel her forehead begin to pulsate as Arthur's dreamy smile expanded. Arthur leaned back in his chair and his face displayed pure ecstasy. Mrs. Harrison's forehead was under immense pressure. She stared intensely at Arthur, her expression bordering on a kind of hatred that no teacher of children should be capable of conjuring. Arthur began flaring his nostrils to the rhythm of "Twinkle, Twinkle Little Star."

Now Mrs. Harrison's nostrils also began to flare. Just when it looked like her head would surely explode, she bolted up from her seat and yelled in a terrible, shrill voice. "ARTHUR!"

Arthur looked up at her blankly. His nostrils became still.

"Yes?" said Arthur.

Mrs. Harrison was unprepared to follow up her outburst. She sputtered something unintelligible and rubbed her forehead with her knuckles. "Get up here right now!" she yelled, pointing to the floor beside her desk.

Arthur walked up to the front of the class and looked at her curiously. The students watched with growing anticipation. This was much better than silent reading.

Mrs. Harrison began scribbling madly on the blackboard. She broke a piece of chalk and picked up a new one. "If you're not going to do the work I assign you," she said through gritted teeth, "I'm going to *make* you work." She finished writing and stepped aside, revealing a lengthy, complicated arithmetic problem.

"There," she said. "You can solve this mathematical problem while the rest of the class continues to read *silently*." She glared at the class, covering them in a thin layer of fear.

She turned back to Arthur. "Silent reading will be over when you complete this problem," she said. The students groaned and reluctantly returned to their books, deflated and disappointed that the altercation had not come to a more confrontational end.

Mrs. Harrison sat back down behind her desk, feeling better, feeling that her world was back in balance. She was in control again. Her pulse slowed and the ocean behind her forehead calmed. She took a deep breath and exhaled slowly.

****

Moments later, Mrs. Harrison glanced at Arthur to see how he was progressing with the math problem. What she saw was Arthur swaying gently back and forth, eyes closed, completely ignoring the math problem. Mrs. Harrison felt something click just behind her forehead. Her eyes bulged. She shot up out of her chair and lunged at Arthur, making a strange gurgling sound like a choking wildcat.

In the very same moment, an errant cloud of chalk dust settled in the air just beneath Arthur's nostrils. As Mrs. Harrison lunged at him, Arthur drew in his breath sharply, sucking the entire cloud of chalk dust deep into his nasal cavity. His nose twitched. His nostrils flared. Just when Mrs. Harrison was nearly on top of him, Arthur turned and sneezed directly into her face.

Mrs. Harrison froze in mid-stride, held up like a statue covered in pigeon poop, except in this case the pigeon poop was little bits of human saliva, mucus and phlegm. Mrs. Harrison flushed red, except for the enormous vein on her forehead, which turned a shade of bright blue that would have been a pretty colour for a birthday cake. A few students began to chuckle cautiously. Mrs. Harrison stumbled. She groped along the wooden edge of her desk with her fingers and fell back into her seat where she began to tremble. The children were no longer afraid. They erupted with laughter. They laughed freely and with greater vigor.

Arthur stood terrified at the front of the class. He was not terrified because of what Mrs. Harrison might do to him, but because he thought he might have sneezed too hard and completely erased his memory. He took a deep breath and tested out his brain: "Genesis! Exodus! Leviticus! Numbers! Deuteronomy!..." The children's laughter grew louder and louder.

****

Four ladies sat in the living room, curtains half-drawn, black fluffy cat lounging on top of the piano, two empty bottles of red wine and a nearly-empty bowl of chocolate chip cookies on the dark wooden coffee table.

Sheila laughed. Jacqueline Snadjman laughed too. Their laughter was not like children's laughter. It was harsher and more distorted. It was impure. It was hard on the ears. It was sharp as a knife, not clear as a bell. Their laughter was not contagious. It was the type of laughter that should not be called laughter at all, really.

Sheila and Jacqueline sat in the sunlit room along with two other ladies whose names are not important. They were dumb, dull ladies who spoke of dumb, dull things. But Jacqueline enjoyed their company because their ears were always open and only too ready to absorb her gossip.

Jacqueline was the host of this little get-together. She was drunk again. Her loud voice had taken charge of the airwaves, bloating with wine, growing louder and louder until it flooded the whole house. The three guests sat back in their chairs and listened as Jacqueline slurred her way through a blurry maze of rose-colored words and hazy wine-inspired thoughts.

"All I'm saying," she slurred, "is that I think game shows are a massive conspiracy, as big a conspiracy as the world has ever known." The two dumb ladies nodded their heads graciously as Sheila let out a laugh. Jacqueline was offended.

"I'm serious," said Jacqueline. "I have reason to believe that game shows are part of a secret government conspiracy to rid the country of all citizens with below average IQs. Haven't you ever wondered why you only see stupid people on gameshows? It's because it's all a façade." She continued speaking very loudly. "It's like the Holocaust all over again, but this time the government is killing the stupid and the ignorant instead of the Jews, and this time they're doing a better job of hiding it."

The ladies didn't dare laugh. They nodded their heads in synchronized approval, shooting careful, eye-rolling glances across the room on hidden wavelengths.

"Think about it," Jacqueline leaned too far forward in her seat and steadied herself with her fingertips on the carpet. "What if game show contestants were never actually given their prizes? What if the government actually took the winners to a secret facility, promising to award them their new boat or new car or whatever, and instead of giving them a prize, just slaughtered them all and hid their bodies in a field?"

One of the dumb ladies, the one with brown hair, spoke up. "Well why should we care if the government gets rid of all the idiots? I say good riddance!" She laughed like a squawking bird, as though she had just said a very funny thing.

The other dumb lady, the one with blonde hair, laughed also, but more like a surprised horse than a squawking bird. "Oh, you are so ruthless!" she said. Her nervous fingers reached up to adjust her tangled blonde hair. The ladies were completely oblivious to how dumb, in fact, they were.

Sheila chuckled and chugged back some more wine. She wiped a dribble from the corner of her purple lips. "But if game shows really are a massive conspiracy to get rid of stupid people, how do you explain Jeopardy? People on that show are pretty smart. Does the government kill them too?"

"Hmmm," Jacqueline squinted. "I suppose Jeopardy would be the exception to the rule." She lifted herself from her chair and teetered towards the kitchen. "Need more wine," she mumbled.

Jacqueline didn't know it at the time, but one day very soon she would cause her best friend Sheila to run away from Turtle Pond forever.

****

Here is another thing Jacqueline did not know: Her best friend Sheila used to be an aspiring short story writer before she decided to get married and forfeit her individual freedom.

Sheila had never published any of her stories, but she still kept them tucked away in a dusty wooden chest in the attic.

One of Sheila's short stories was about an earth-like planet in a far-off galaxy. The planet was called Medica and it was almost exactly like earth. The only difference was that Medica had only one chain of Chinese Restaurant. It was called Wong's Wok. Wong's Wok was everywhere. There was literally a Wong's Wok on every other street corner. Some people ate at Wong's every night of the week. There were a lot of fat people on Medica, just like on earth.

After you finished eating a meal at Wong's Wok, a friendly Chinese boy or a beautiful Chinese girl would come out from the kitchen and give a fortune cookie to everyone at your table. The boy's name would most likely be "Eric," and the girl's name would probably be "Lisa."

All the fat people at the table would break open their fortune cookies and read the words on the little slips of paper inside. Here is what they read: "Beware of sharp knives", "Beware of falling elevators", "Beware of fast-moving vehicles", "Beware of people who are different than you", and so on.

After eating at Wong's Wok, the fat people would return home, lock their front doors and tuck themselves into bed. Many people had trouble sleeping at night because of all the ominous things they had read on the little slips of paper.

Eventually, all the smart people on Medica stopped eating at Wong's Wok altogether. These people stayed at home and cooked their own food. Their food was colorful and healthy, and the people enjoyed being in the kitchen, mixing ingredients and creating their own recipes.

But there was a strange attraction that kept bringing certain people back to Wong's Wok night after night. Some people suspected that Wong's Wok put addictive ingredients in their food, and they were probably right.

So a majority of Medicanites continued eating at Wong's, growing fatter and fatter, reading the little slips of paper, and returning home terrified of everything around them. These people didn't know that what the fortune cookies told them was not true or honest. They didn't know what the smart people knew, that the fortune cookies were made by thoughtless metal robots without souls.

****

The lazy sun rested high above Turtle Pond. Were it to suddenly fall from the sky, it appeared it would land squarely in the middle of town.

Jim stretched out across the sofa like a lanky, balding cat. Luckily for him, the couch was located outside (inside), so he was safe from the dangers of a falling sun. Arthur and Karl were still at school and Sheila was at Jacqueline Snadjman's house. They wouldn't be home for at least a couple more hours.

Jim wasn't wearing any pants. He turned on the TV and a children's show about a clumsy Spanish-speaking dragon appeared on the screen. The dragon *was* wearing pants. "That's strange," said Jim.

It was 11:00am and Jim was considering taking his first nap of the day. He would normally be at work at this time of day, but the employees of Happy Steel Co. had decided to go on strike and today was the first day. Jim had forgotten to tell Sheila about the strike. He made a mental note to tell her when she got home.

Happy Steel Co. was a steel plant located just a few miles outside of Turtle Pond. The owner and president was a man by the name of Miso Happy, a very rich businessman who moved to Turtle Pond from China. Mr. Happy was known to be a very greedy man. It's rumoured that before he moved to Turtle Pond, Mr. Happy had traded his only daughter for a gold watch and a set of stainless steel pots and pans.

****

The employees of Happy Steel Co. weren't happy with what they were being paid. They decided to go on strike until Mr. Happy agreed to increase their wages. A month ago they would never have dreamed of going on strike. But then Mr. Happy raised the retail price of all steel products by $5 per ton without also raising the wages of his employees. The employees were outraged when they learned of the increase, claiming that Mr. Happy, and the government, who was working in conjunction with Mr. Happy, were profiting while the workers' wages stayed the same.

So a handful of disgruntled workers banded together to form the "Union of Happy Workers," or "Un.Happy" for short. They created a list of demands and gave them to Mr. Happy. Here were their demands:

1) Minimum 17.5 cent/hour wage increase for all employees
2) Mandatory 2 weeks paid vacation after 2 years of employment
3) Minimum 3 smoke breaks a day
4) A snack bar fully stocked with cigarettes, drinks, and an assortment of junk food

They were really shooting for the stars!

****

Mr. Happy, being the greedy, penny-pinching man that he was, refused to comply with Un.Happy's demands. So all 227 employees took a vote, and when the ballots were counted, it was found that all but one employee had voted to go on strike.

The only employee who voted against the strike was 78-year-old Leonard Frankfurt. Leonard was perfectly content receiving a paycheck, however large or small, for doing nothing but sweeping bits of metal and dust off the factory floors.

Leonard was going to die soon anyways. He would be run over by a stolen car driven by a woman even older than he was.

****

Jim stared blankly at the television. The clumsy Spanish dragon sneezed and accidentally burned down an entire Mexican village. He blushed and flew clumsily back to his cave. Jim looked down and studied his naked, bony shins. When he was a young man his calves had been muscular and well defined. Where had his calves gone? He let out a heavy sigh.

Jim didn't know it at the time but he was about to view a TV commercial that would change his life.

CHAPTER 5

"To be famous, in fact, one has only to kill one's landlady." – *Albert Camus*

****

Mr. Matthews thought that filling his students' heads with imaginative lies was better than teaching them how to become analogous, indoctrinated, responsible adults, capable of seamlessly integrating into a broken society.

Mr. Matthews once wrote a book called "The Dangers of Kindness." The picture on the front cover was a bright yellow sun with a bold, red X slashing through it. He had published the book five years ago, but had yet to sell a single copy, probably because all the pages inside were blank.

****

It seems so simple. Our only job is to be kind.

****

And then Mr. Matthews said the thing that would change Karl's life forever. Here is what he said: "I urge you to ask and answer life's deepest questions as though your existence depends on it, because the answers to those questions may be the very things upon which your soul hangs."

****

Why was Mr. Matthews saying such things to a bunch of 9-year-old kids? My best guess is that he enjoyed shaping the minds of young people into deep wells of curiosity, even if they ended up being extremely confused 90% of the time.

Whatever.

When Mr. Matthews uttered this single sentence, this seemingly harmless sentence about being brave and courageous and honest and facing reality head-on, something clicked inside Karl's head. Whatever clicked was now locked into a new, permanent position.

Karl stood up and walked through (out) the door. Mr. Matthews smiled and didn't try to stop him.

****

Lining the walls of Turtle Pond Elementary School was a series of large white posters boasting slogans like, "No Hugging!" and "Physical contact will NOT be tolerated!" They were part of a new campaign by the Teachers Union to stop children from touching each other.

You see, the teachers were sick of seeing little boys playing tag with other little boys. They were sick of seeing little girls hugging other little girls. They were especially sick of seeing little girls hugging little boys. How angry that made them. Many of the more sponge-faced, bitter-mouthed, muddy-eyed teachers wore round pins on their shirts boasting slogans like, "Stop The Hugging!" or "Zero Tolerance!"

****

Karl was in such a daze that he no longer noticed the posters on the walls. He no longer felt his legs moving as they carried him down the school hallway towards the front door. He was fully absorbed in the repercussions of the single sentence that had just escaped Mr. Matthew's lips. Karl walked past the giant mural of two sad children holding hands. He walked right past the mural and through (out) the front door.

Karl didn't know it at the time, but his next visit to Turtle Pond School would also be his last.

****

Fact: Patti LaVernon's parents were both blind. Mother blind and father blind. Blind as bats.

Fact: Patti LaVernon had been born with perfect 20/20 vision.

Fact: Patti LaVernon was, without question, the coolest girl in school. She had it all- the looks, the attitude, the grades, the money, the legion of devoted friends. This is why Arthur was so shocked when Patti tapped him on the shoulder at recess.

Arthur looked up from the ant hill he had been intently studying. He saw Patti LaVernon and his face flushed red. His heart fluttered. To Arthur, love felt a lot like a heart murmur.

"Hey Arthur," said Patti. "You've got a lot of guts standing up to Mrs. Harrison like that. Everybody's talking about it, you know."

This was news to Arthur. Nobody had said a word to him since he sneezed on Mrs. Harrison that morning.

Patti shook her head in disbelief. "I can't believe you yelled out all the books of the Bible right in Mrs. Harrison's face. Especially when everybody knows she's a diehard atheist."

Arthur didn't know what the word atheist meant, but he felt a ball of pride growing in his chest for having impressed Patti LaVernon, the coolest girl in school. He opened his mouth to say something but nothing came out.

"Anyways," said Patti, "I'm having a few people over to my house after school tomorrow. You should come." She hesitated, "I mean, if you're not busy or anything."

Arthur wasn't sure if Patti was asking him or ordering him. He managed to nod his head.

"Great," said Patti. She turned and walked back to her group of admiring followers.

A grin slowly spread across Arthur's face. Things were finally starting to turn around for him. He was finally starting to fit in. Thank God he could recite all the books of the Bible!

****

Minor insignificant detail: Arthur was named after the character "Fonzie" from the television show *Happy Days*, whose full name was Arthur Fonzarelli. On Arthur's 10th birthday, his father Jim had given him a leather jacket. It was two sizes too large and made Arthur look even skinnier than he already was, but he wore the jacket every single day just to make Jim happy. It had been 255 days since Arthur's 10th birthday.

****

The television was yelling at Jim. It was making fun of him, telling him he was worthless and then offering him shiny objects to medicate his destroyed self-esteem.

A bearded man was telling Jim to buy his product. It could have been any product. Jim snorted and reached for the converter to turn off the television. And then the commercial that would change Jim's life forever appeared on the screen.

"Do you love shampoo?" a man's voice yelled at Jim from inside the television. The man had a strong Italian accent. Jim's thumb froze on top of the red power button.

"Do you love chocolate?" the sexy Italian voice asked Jim. Jim sat up on the couch and stared at the television.

"Yes," said Jim, "I do."

"Then you're going to love Vivacious

Vincenzo's Special Shampoo Formula For Men. It will make your head smell like a fresh batch of brownies. Just watch!" The commercial had Jim's full attention.

The screen blinked to an upper body shot of a man taking a shower. The man was eating a soggy brownie with one hand and massaging a thick brown substance into his hair with the other. His facial expression displayed pure bliss. He was grinning and moaning as though someone was fondling his private parts just below the frame.

The screen blinked again. The same man was now kneeling down in the middle of a sparkling white kitchen. Atop his head was a carefully balanced stack of steaming brownies. A middle-aged woman and three ugly children, supposedly the man's family, stood around him, gleefully rubbing their hands together and licking their lips while staring at the brownies. The man fought off a grimace. He was in pain due to the pile of steaming brownies on top of his head.

"Mmmm, smell those freshly-baked, warm, gooey brownies," said the sexy Italian voice.

The man in the kitchen took the platter of brownies off of his head and threw it onto the floor.

"Those aren't brownies you smell," said the man. "That's my hair!"

On cue, the family looked up at the camera and flashed simultaneous cheesy smiles. The screen froze on their smiling faces and the sexy Italian voice blurted out, "Vivacious Vincenzo's Special Shampoo Formula For Men is a trademark of Vivacious Vincenzo Inc. and is only sold at Vivacious Vincenzo's Shampoo Emporium in the city of Paxton. For a limited time only. Come get yours today!"

The commercial was over. Jim turned off the television and sat stunned on the couch, his jaw hanging open. He felt like he had just stumbled upon a treasure chest, like he was in the middle of a wonderful dream, like his life finally had a purpose. He felt that Vivacious Vincenzo had created a product just for him, combining his two favorite things in the world- brownies and shampoo- into a single bottle of bubbly brown liquid joy.

Lately Jim had been experiencing the initial pangs of an existential mid-life crisis, but now he forgot all about his worries. Here is what Jim was thinking as he sat there on the couch: *If only I could get my hands on a bottle of Vivacious Vincenzo's Special Shampoo Formula For Men, I could die a happy man.*

****

"I could die a happy man." That doesn't make a speck of sense. Nobody in the history of mankind has died happy. Not one person. No one is happy to die.

Jesus? He died willingly, dutifully, lovingly, but certainly not happily. "My God, why have you forsaken me?"

The Buddhist monk who set himself on fire in the name of peace and freedom? He did not die happy. The second he set himself on fire all he could feel was the searing pain of fire melting his skin. The pain blurred his senses as he sat there like a statue. There was no room left to feel anything else, not even regret for having set himself on fire.

What about the man in the electric chair whose last words were, "Well this will certainly teach me a lesson"? He died with a sharp sense of irony and wit. But being clearheaded as he was, he could not have been happy about the straps around his limbs or the electric hat that was placed atop his shaven, water-soaked head.

Those who commit suicide? They do not die happy. Many of them are too sad to live.

****

Suicide is an interesting phenomenon. Albert Camus wrote, "There is but one truly serious philosophical problem, and that is suicide." He was not suggesting that we should spend great amounts of time contemplating suicide, but that we should spend a great amount of time disproving suicide by truly living. He went on to explain, "Judging whether life is or is not worth living amounts to answering the fundamental question of philosophy." Albert Camus did not want us to stay alive. He wanted us to *LIVE*.

****

Imagine we had undeniable scientific proof that some form of afterlife exists, though we did not know what it was like. Perhaps then the term "committing suicide" would be replaced by something more upbeat and humane; something with more positive connotations, like "going for gold" or "fast-tracking" or "solving the mystery."

****

Do animals commit suicide? No. Animals don't commit suicide. We get to them first.

****

It comforts people to think that there is an afterlife. The notion that we will live on in another world after we die makes it easier to deal with death, and with life.

I would not prevent you from wearing a warm blanket, nor would I stop you from thinking comforting thoughts. Just please try not to use your blanket to strangle anyone.

****

"I'm a winner," says the millionaire. "I'm a loser," says the millionaire on his deathbed.

****

Jacqueline's limp, wine-infused body lay passed out, stretched across the couch. Dumb lady #1 had gone home. Dumb lady #2 was throwing up in the bathroom sink.

Sheila leaned forward, amid stillness and silence, and poured herself another glass of wine. She gazed out the window and the afternoon sun burned her pupils. She closed her eyes and thought about what her life had become. If everything had gone to plan, she would be in Paris right now, living in a small apartment, unmarried, with no children, eating baguettes and writing stories about her adventures and the people she met on her travels. A female Henry Miller. Her wistful thoughts were interrupted by the sound of puke splashing on porcelain.

****

One of Sheila's short stories was set in the year 2132. It took place in the world's first and only "brain swap clinic" in New York City. People went to the brain swap clinic to experience what it feels like to use someone else's brain for a few moments. It was a brand new procedure and it was extravagantly expensive. Since it was a brain *swap* clinic, visitors were required to bring a friend or a spouse or a neighbor to swap brains with.

When a pair of visitors arrived at the clinic, they were split up into two adjacent white rooms. In between the rooms was a thin white wall with a small round hole near the bottom where bundles of colorful wires ran through. The visitors had their heads dunked into a large vat of glowing green gel and were hooked up to a bunch of suction cups, nodes, wires and doohickeys. The operator counted down, "3,2,1," the switch was flipped and the clients' brains were swapped.

Brain swap sessions were available in intervals of 1 minute, 3 minutes or 5 minutes. Scientists claimed that if a person swapped brains for any longer than five minutes they risked causing permanent damage to their cerebral cortex and could end up a vegetable for the rest of their life. The scientists explained that after five minutes of experiencing another person's brain, the human body assumes it won't be going back to the old brain and starts making changes throughout the body-recalibrating connections and reflexes, creating new systems, rewiring hardware, and severing neural pathways that are impossible to rebuild.

Apparently the functioning of our brains is beyond our control. Our brains are much better off without our interference.

At the time, the New York brain swap clinic was being touted as the solution to all the world's problems. It would put a stop to the war and destruction and hatred that had plagued mankind since we were first molded from mud or whatever. Scientists had discovered that swapping brains, even for a few seconds, caused a fundamental change in the way people thought and functioned. It created what some scientists were calling a "6th sense." Brain swaps allowed people to relate to one another on a deeply empathetic level that had never before been possible. It allowed people to walk in somebody else's shoes, to literally test-drive somebody else's brain.

Prominent New York Times columnist, Peter Szweller, wrote about the brain swap clinic in his weekly column, saying, "People enter as friends and leave as soulmates."

There were some, though, who hated the brain swap clinic because it made them feel stupid and average. You see, many visitors were shocked to find out that there was very little difference between their brain and the brain of their friend or spouse or neighbor.

It wasn't uncommon for a visitor to be

strapped in and hooked up, and after experiencing another person's brain for two minutes, ask, "Is it turned on yet?"

Many people asked for a refund.

****

The brain swap clinic story came to an end when a husband and wife visited the clinic. The husband brought his wife there to celebrate their 5th anniversary. He thought the brain swap experience would strengthen their crumbling relationship, and perhaps stave off the seemingly inevitable divorce for a few more years.

The husband was a loudmouth car salesman and the wife sold earrings made out of seashells. The husband was anxious to get the brain swap over with so he and his wife could go home and be madly in love again, just like they were five years ago.

They were led to their adjacent white rooms, their heads were dunked into large vats of glowing green gel, they were hooked up to all sorts of suction cups, nodes, wires and doohickeys. The operator counted down, "3,2,1." The switch was flipped. Nothing happened. The man was confused. Was the machine broken?

A moment later his head began to vibrate violently. His mouth shot open and he began quoting Shakespeare uncontrollably. "Love looks not with the eyes but with the mind." His eyes opened wider than they ever had before.

"O, what men dare do!" he yelled. "What men may do! What men daily do, not knowing what they do!" He saw bright colors and patterns flashing before his eyes and he heard the clear beautiful music of harps, bells and angel choirs all around him.

"He's mad that trusts in the tameness of a wolf, a horse's health, a boy's love, or a whore's oath." Numbers and letters danced before his eyes. He bolted upright on the table.

"Though this be madness, yet there is method in't." His head felt like it was being squeezed in a vice. His voice grew louder and louder.

"What a piece of work is a man, how noble in reason, how infinite in faculties, in form and moving how express and admirable, in action how like an angel, in apprehension how like a god!"

In the next room, the man's wife lay quietly on the table, not moving, staring straight up at the white ceiling. A single small tear escaped the corner of her eye and trickled down the landscape of her cheek. She could hear her husband yelling in the next room, but she felt paralyzed, helpless, lazy. She could not bring herself to care about anything. She had a strange craving to drink beer.

The man's head felt pressurized, bloated, like an egg about to explode in the sun. He became enraged. He was enraged because even in the midst of the swap, his "self" somehow realized that his wife's brain was better, faster, and superior to his. Her brain far exceeded his brain's capabilities.

How dare she!

The husband gripped a handful of wires and ripped the suction cups from his body. He teetered over to the towering computer in the center of the room and heaved his shoulder against it. It gave way and timbered over, crashing to the ground with a metallic bang, sending sparks dancing in all directions.

"There was never yet a philosopher that could endure the toothache patiently!" he screamed.

He kicked the computer's control board, the part with the most flashing lights and buttons, the testicles of the computer. The computer burst into flames. Red lights flashed and alarm bells rang as white-coated workers swarmed into the room.

Moments later, the entire brain swap clinic lay in ruins. It was completely burned to the ground. Not a single thing was salvaged.

The worst part about it was that it was impossible to replace the brain swap technology because the inventor had died two months earlier and had left no blueprints behind.

People all around the world were devastated.

Needless to say, the wife was pretty ticked off at her husband for destroying the world's only brain swap clinic and all of its priceless, irreplaceable technology.

So she divorced him.

****

It is a little known fact that angels are actually quite shy. This is why you will never hear an angel singing alone. They only sing in choirs.

CHAPTER 6

"I want to be with those who know secret things or else alone." – *Rainer Maria Rilke*

****

The three oldest living people in the world are all women. They were each asked what the secret to their longevity was. The first woman said she drinks goat's milk every day. The second woman said she eats oatmeal every day. The third woman said she eats cottage cheese every day. This is true. This is not a joke.

****

There is a story about three men who were caught in the middle of a violent thunderstorm. Two of the men were struck by lightning and killed instantly but the third man remained unharmed. When asked how he managed to survive, the third man said, "I ate cottage cheese every day."

****

Karl was on his way to visit Joan Bardchuck. Joan Bardchuck was old and feeble, and awkwardly creepy in a way that only elderly people can be. She was probably the oldest person in Turtle Pond, though nobody knew for sure.

Joan's bulging, veiny eyes were deep-set within bowl-like sockets and always accentuated with a distasteful amount of makeup. Her facial features were sharp and skeletal with an almost-translucent, flimsy sheet of dry wrinkled skin draped carelessly across her face. It was a wonder her knife-like zygomatic bones didn't poke identical holes through her cheeks.

Karl's only previous interaction with Joan had been at the grocery store two months earlier. Joan had bent over to pick up a box of unsalted crackers from the bottom shelf, and had let out a dry, whiffy fart just as Karl walked behind her.

Joan had turned and apologized to Karl. She waved her hand through the lingering stench in the air.

"I've got to stop eating eggs for breakfast," she said.

Joan was far too old to be embarrassed by any kind of involuntary bodily function, and this display of confidence had impressed Karl. It was because of her age and apparent wisdom that Karl chose to seek out her opinion first.

****

Sidenote: Karl had been shocked to discover that elderly people's farts actually smell like potpourri. Some young entrepreneur could bottle the stuff and sell it back to the unsuspecting elderly population as perfume. The difficult part would be working out the logistics of how to bottle elderly people's farts.

****

Joan's living room reeked of cat-litter and potpourri. Karl tried not to breathe through his nose.

"So, how old are you?" asked Joan.

"I'm ten years old," said Karl.

"And what grade are you in?"

"Grade 3."

"And what's your favorite subject?"

"I'm not sure." Karl scanned the room and raised his eyebrows. Apparently Joan was an avid collector of ducks. Not real ducks, but duck ornaments and trinkets. Her shelves, tables, bookcases and windowsills were lined with rows and rows of ducks. Fat ducks, skinny ducks, mother ducks, baby ducks, multi-colored ducks, ducks stacked on top of ducks.

Karl made a mental note: *She must like ducks.*

One must seriously question the sanity and judgment of a person who collects duck ornaments. If you run across one of these people, be careful.

"Enough small talk," said Joan. "To what do I owe the pleasure of your company?"

"Well," said Karl. "I'm trying to find out what a permanium is."

"Oh!" Joan jerked forward and splashed tea onto her lap. She frowned down at the spot on her blouse and rubbed at it with her frail, arthritic fingers. She stood up and walked to the kitchen, giving Karl a worried look as she went.

"You don't want to know what a permanium is," Joan called back to Karl through the open kitchen door. "Trust me."

"But I *do* want to know what a permanium

is." Karl sat quietly for a moment. "That's the *only* thing I want to know."

Joan emerged from the kitchen with a large blurry stain on her blouse. She huffed as she sat down.

"Well, I'm sure permaniums are nice enough," she said. "But let's just say that if I was a pregnant mother and I knew that my child was going to be a permanium, I would have an abortion."

"What's an abortion?" asked Karl.

Joan smiled at the poor ignorant child.

Karl felt sick to his stomach.

"An abortion is something we do to make sure that ugly, weirdo babies don't get born," said Joan.

"Oh," said Karl. "So is it like killing babies?"

Joan thought for a moment. "It's more like killing *baby* babies."

Karl frowned.

"Don't worry," Joan reassured him. "We just have to let people kill baby babies for a little while longer. In the future we'll be able to cure all the ugly, weirdo babies before they're born. No one will ever have to give birth to a freak baby again."

"How will we do that?" asked Karl.

"Science, my dear," said Joan. "Science."

Karl frowned harder. "That's all very interesting," he said, "but I still want to know what a permanium is."

Joan looked at Karl with pity and growing frustration in her veiny red eyes. "Trust me honey," she said, "you don't want to know."

Joan moistened her biscuit in her tea and took a bite. She chewed the mushy biscuit noisily and Karl cringed.

The only thing in the world that made Karl angry was when people chewed their food loudly. More specifically, when people chewed their food and the food moved up and down between their tongue and the roof of their mouth, becoming stuck and unstuck repeatedly, making an unbearable squishing noise like the soft *cluck* of a chicken.

Karl suddenly didn't feel so good. He needed fresh air. He was not going to find any answers here.

Joan was busy readjusting her dentures and didn't notice Karl as he stood up and walked through (out) the door.

What neither of them knew was that Joan, a fearful homophobe, had mistaken the word permanium for the word homosexual.

****

Mr. Matthews had once told Karl's class that the wisest living thing on earth was an unborn human fetus. He told them that an unborn fetus contains all the world's knowledge and wisdom inside its tiny little unborn head, and that all that knowledge and wisdom is instantly internalized deep into the brain's core at the exact moment of birth.

The rest of our time on earth, according to Mr. Matthews, is spent attempting to uncover and repossess all that buried knowledge and wisdom using the tools we have been given: our eyes, ears, nose, hands, and sometimes our mouth.

****

Arthur had always thought that the tallest man in the world should be declared the "Emperor of the World." He had subconsciously taken note that taller men were treated with more respect, were considered more important, and were generally higher on the societal scale of power than shorter men.

Arthur had once mentioned this idea about the tall "Emperor of the World" to Mrs. Harrison and she had laughed right in his face.

"That's great Arthur," she said. "Now please take your seat and finish your assignment."

****

There is a point to all this. I'm sure of it.

****

Here's another thing Mr. Matthews said to his sleepy class one day:

"You know what I don't understand about evolution? Why didn't everything evolve into humans? Why did turtles evolve into turtles? How can a three-toed sloth possibly be the evolutionary peak of a species? Why didn't cats grow long giraffe-legs so they could eat apples out of trees? Why didn't dogs stand up like humans, develop consciousness, and invent arithmetic and the automobile?" Mr. Matthews stared out at his students.

"More importantly, if evolution is real, why do farts still smell bad?" He paused thoughtfully.

"Our thoughts, our ideas, our consciousness is quite meaningless since it's stuck inside this language and these words that we created ourselves and gave meaning to," Mr. Matthews was pacing back and forth behind his desk.

"Our words mean absolutely nothing to any species but our own. Our language has self-prescribed itself as meaningful. Our language, our traditions, our beliefs, all of it is like a painting of a painting of a painting that, as it moves backwards in time, keeps getting smaller and smaller until *poof!* it disappears."

****

"And think about this..." Mr. Matthews wasn't finished yet. "Isn't it strange that all animals have mouths that they use to eat food? And isn't it strange that all animals poop out of their butt? And what's really strange is that all animals' butts look the same. And the same goes for eyeballs. Isn't it strange that an elephant's eyeball is so similar to a human's eyeball? Doesn't that seem just a little bit strange to you? Think about it. Seriously, think about it."

****

What a waste of breath. What a waste of energy.

****

Mr. Matthews had once posed the following question to his grade two class, concerning the idea of Creationism:

"What came first, the woman or the male organ?"

Most of the young students had been confused or disgusted, but Karl had to admit it was a very good question. Did Adam have a plug before there was a hole?

****

I cannot emphasize how little we know, how much we do not know, and how much we pretend to know.

****

Human progress is as fast as a speeding glacier. Perhaps slower.

CHAPTER 7

"I want to prevent as many men as possible from pretending that they have to do this or that because they must earn a living. *It is not true*. One can starve to death- it is much better." – Henry Miller

****

The clouds rose vertically in the sky, mushrooming upwards, stemming from a barrage of unseen midair explosions. Somewhere up there, beyond the clouds, invisible angels waged warfare against evil spirits using foam swords and water guns. God relaxed in his housecoat and slippers, watching the battle and cheering on the angels from his sofa.

Sheila was washing dishes in the kitchen while Jim, Arthur and Karl watched television in the living room. This was their nightly post-dinner tradition: Sheila washed dishes while Jim and the boys watched television.

On top of doing the dishes Sheila also vacuumed, dusted, made lunch, did the laundry, made dinner, cleaned the cat litter, and so on. She even collected Jim's dirty socks from the floor, washed them, folded them, and returned them to his dresser. Sheila never complained about any of this. That's just how things were.

Some women might claim that Sheila shouldn't be doing all the house chores while Jim sat around watching television. Some women might claim that the female gender is being oppressed by patriarchal, horrible, bigoted men. They might be right. But a lot of those same women fall in love with patriarchal, horrible, bigoted men and end up cleaning their dirty socks for them while they sit around and watch television.

It's all very confusing.

****

Sheila had a salty cotton ball lodged in her throat. She made an awkward choking sound and steadied herself against the kitchen counter.

"You want to know *what*?"

"I want to know what a permanium is," said Karl.

Sheila stammered and her face blanched white.

"I thought you'd be the best person to ask, Mom," said Karl. "But if you don't know what a permanium is, that's okay."

Sheila opened her mouth to speak, but before she could say anything, Jim called out from the living room.

"Sheila! Karl! Come quick!" yelled Jim. "Mayor Cotton is about to make an announcement!"

Karl shrugged and strolled into the living room, leaving Sheila silent and alone with her spinning thoughts. Did Karl know her secret? Could he have figured it out?

Sheila's head throbbed with the pressurized worry of a new danger that could be neither confirmed nor denied.

No. Impossible! Nobody knew her secret.

Her mind screamed and lashed out in all directions. She tried to calm herself.

Forget it. It's just a coincidence. There's nothing to worry about.

****

Mayor Cotton's round face filled the television screen. His gray hair shimmered in the spotlight, reminding Jim of the shampoo commercial he had seen earlier that afternoon.

"Good evening citizens of Turtle Pond."

Mayor Cotton sat behind a dark mahogany desk and spoke into a pair of criss-crossed black microphones. "I would like to begin by offering my sincerest apologies to Reynold Reynoldson for the events that occurred on the Turtle Pond Morning News Program this morning. The words and actions of Bull Whalelike were inappropriate and regrettable. I'd like to apologize to you, Reynold, on behalf of Turtle Pond." Mayor Cotton paused and adjusted his purple necktie.

"You know," he said, "it's not easy being a permanium. We must try to understand and appreciate how much pain these people go through. We must help them out every way we can. Permaniums did not ask to be born permaniums, just like blind people did not ask to be born blind." Mayor Cotton spoke with conviction and empathy, his brow crumpling with wavy canyons.

"Permaniums do not lead easy lives. They cannot live freely like you and I. No, permaniums must constantly be aware of what they eat and drink. They cannot lose concentration even for a moment, or they may end up inadvertently drinking a juice box or eating a slice of cake that could potentially kill them. And furthermore, those little needles they have to keep pricking themselves with are very painful."

Apparently, Mayor Cotton had confused a permanium with a person who had diabetes.

"And so," he continued, "in order to create some much-needed awareness of this important issue, and to honour our hero, Reynold Reynoldson, I officially declare the next seven days to be Turtle Pond's "First Annual Permanium Awareness Week!"

Jim, Sheila, Arthur and Karl sat in stunned silence.

"For the next seven days we will be celebrating the amazing achievements and the unique culture of some of our most outstanding permanium citizens. I hope you will all show your support and do your part in creating awareness. And if there are any permaniums out there watching right now, I'd like to invite you to come down to City Hall where we have a special surprise for you." Mayor Cotton winked, and Sheila shuddered.

"Thank you all, and good night."

Jim flicked off the TV.

"Whaddya know," said Jim. He rubbed his balding head. He was thinking about Vivacious Vincenzo's shampoo.

"That's exciting," said Arthur. He sneezed. He was thinking about Patti LaVernon, the coolest girl in school.

Karl didn't say anything. He was eight years old and was not expected to have an opinion. He was more confused than ever about what a permanium was.

"Huh," grunted Sheila. She knew deep down that the town could not possibly be tolerant of permaniums.

Sheila's secret was under threat, and she was going to have to guard it with her life. She was horrified, scared stiff of what the townspeople would do to her if they found out she was a permanium.

****

You see, Sheila thought this whole Permanium Awareness Week thing was a trap. She thought it was a stunt headed up by Mayor Cotton and his cronies to systematically exterminate all the permaniums in town.

She had seen the evil gleam in his eyes as he made his announcement. She knew Mayor Cotton wanted her to turn herself in, and that is precisely what she would not do.

****

Jim, Sheila, Arthur and Karl did not know it at the time, but this was the last time they would ever be together as a family.

While everybody else was getting ready for bed, Jim sat alone on the couch, staring at his reflection in the blank television screen.

"Are you coming to bed, dear?" Sheila called down from the top of the stairs.

"In a bit, dear," Jim called back.

"Okay. Good night, dear."

"Good night, dear."

Pause.

"Good night Dad."

"Good night Arthur."

"Good night Dad."

"Good night Karl."

Jim listened for the click of three bedroom doors. He flicked off the light and waited for ten minutes, and then snuck silently through (out) the back door into the darkness.

CHAPTER 8

"Peace on earth would mean the end of civilization as we know it." – *Joseph Heller*

****

People only begin to care about a particular disease and search for a cure after a well-known celebrity or pubic figure has contracted it. Or, if half the world contracts the disease, then there is a high probability that people will begin to care about it and search for a cure. But this is not guaranteed. It all depends on how many rich, white people are affected.

****

It was the day after Mayor Cotton announced Permanium Awareness Week, and the people of Turtle Pond had already made signs, banners, buttons, t-shirts and bumper stickers that boasted slogans like, "We are all permaniums on the inside," and "Honk if you love permaniums."

One lady made t-shirts with the words, "I'm with permanium" printed on the front with an arrow pointing sideways.

To be honest, Mayor Cotton could have declared it "Underpants Awareness Week" and the townspeople would have responded with equal enthusiasm and well-intentioned ignorance.

****

Well-Intentioned Ignorance: the beauty and innocence we see in animals; the main ingredient in a peaceful world; the incapacity to harbour bad intentions; what we humans will never have because our brains are too large and we think too much.

Our good intentions are constantly burdened by knowledge.

****

Though nobody knew it at the time, the only other permanium in Turtle Pond besides Reynold Reynoldson was Sheila. Since Reynold Reynoldson had skipped town the previous night, Sheila was now the only permanium left in town.

CHAPTER 9

"Discourse on virtue and they pass by in droves. Whistle and dance and shimmy, and you've got an audience." – *Diogenes*

****

"Ain't it a shame, we learn and learn and die. Ain't it a shame, we learn and learn and die.

Ain't it a shame, we learn and learn and die..."

This is what Groggy Gary was muttering when Karl found him sitting alone on the curb. Gary was repeating this sentence over and over like some sort of homeless swami uttering his mantra. His words evaporated, dark and smoky, into the glowing atoms just beyond his lips.

Gary's eyes flashed with dull fireworks, wild wonder, and colorful pills. His tangled beard was fit for a family of small birds to comfortably nest in for the winter. His face was dirty like a child's face after playing in the sandbox, or like a soldier's face after playing on the battlefield. Gary's nose slanted sharply to the right side of his face and his mouth to the left side, as though his nose and mouth were repulsed by one another and sought out the furthest corners of his face just to get away.

"Hey, Gary," said Karl.

Gary did not respond, but continued to rock back and forth. Karl saw that Gary's jacket was badly damaged and nearly torn in half across the back.

"Looks like you need a new jacket, Gary," said Karl. "My dad has an extra one. I can go get it for you if you'd like."

"This jacket is fine, thanks," said Gary, not looking up. "I don't care if it's dirty and ripped. I don't give a jumping shit about the clothes people wear. You can put me in a suit and give me glasses but that don't mean I'm smart."

Groggy Gary huffed and kicked at a cigarette butt. His big toe jutted out of a hole in the front of his shoe. Dried blood clung to his broken toenail like month-old nail polish.

"Shoot, I could trade clothes with the

President of the United States, but he'd still be the President and I'd still be a bum."

Groggy Gary continued to mutter to himself under his breath. He rocked forwards and trapped his head between his knees.

Karl sat down next to him. "Yeah, but then you'd be a bum with a nice suit," said Karl. "Maybe then you could get a job and things would get better for you."

Gary sighed and looked up at Karl. Something in Groggy Gary's eyes reminded Karl of the time he had stayed up all night with his sick cat as it slowly died.

Gary lowered his head back down. "No, no, no. Fashion is such a silly joke. It's just another thing we humans make up and call meaningful in order to make ourselves seem better than everybody else. What a silly, silly joke. Take a walk through a leaf-covered forest and then we'll talk about fashion. How about that? We'll see if you can talk about anything after that."

As Gary stared down into the filthy gutter, the sun's rays reflected off the sewer water and illuminated his face.

"Look how the sun shines, Gary," said Karl. "Look how it shines deep into the gutter but never loses its brightness."

****

If Jesus had talked about fashion in the Sermon on the Mount, here is what he might have said: "High class is the lowest class."

****

For Groggy Gary, the best day of the year was Halloween because that was the only day he could fit in with everybody else. His dirty clothes blended in with the cheap costumes, and the mud on his face disguised as make-up.

Every year on Halloween, Groggy Gary would get up out of the gutter and make his way from door to door collecting candy. It was the only day people stopped ignoring him long enough to smile at him and talk to him, to treat him like a human.

What Groggy Gary didn't realize was that everyone knew that the 40-year old trick-or-treater dressed as a homeless man and reeking of whisky was Groggy Gary, but they all gave him candy anyways.

Sometimes when people opened the door and saw Gary standing there with his hands outstretched, they would say, "Oh! And what are you supposed to be?"

Groggy Gary would laugh maniacally, and say, "Why, can't you see? I'm a poor homeless man."

Every Halloween, Groggy Gary could be seen scurrying down the sidewalk, giggling and muttering to himself with a crazy grin on his face, his pockets bulging full of candy.

Groggy Gary also had a homeless cousin named Drunk Andrew who lived in Paxton and used to tell Gary all about his Halloween adventures. Paxton was a bustling town with a few seedy bars and pubs on its main street. On Halloween, Drunk Andrew would sneak into some of these bars and pubs pretending to be an average, house-owning citizen who had dressed up as a bum for Halloween.

While inside, Drunk Andrew would be showered with compliments. People would slap him on the back, shove cups of whiskey and rum into his dirty, groping hands and say things like, "Hey is that real garbage in your hair?" or, "Great costume! That must have cost you a bundle!" or, "Wow! That almost looks like a real puke stain on your shirt," and so on.

One time, Drunk Andrew actually won the "Best Costume" contest and was awarded a coupon for $10 off at a local clothing store. Unfortunately, he was never able to make use of his prize since he was not permitted to enter the store.

Yes, Halloween is a joyous occasion for the homeless.

****

Karl was planning to ask Gary what a permanium was, but decided it was best not to bother him.

****

After school the next day, Patti LaVernon and her friends walked together to Patti's house.

Arthur trailed along a few steps behind the group, content to follow along and listen to their voices as they talked and laughed. Arthur could not believe he was going to Patti LaVernon's house. He did his best to keep calm and cool, but on the inside he was bursting with joy and nervous anticipation.

Did Patti LaVernon like him? Maybe she was in love with him! Maybe they would get married one day and Patti would let Arthur hang out with her more often. Arthur pinched himself on the arm to make sure he wasn't dreaming. He looked up to make sure none of Patti's friends were looking at him. They weren't. They were still talking and laughing. Arthur could have taken off his pants and worn them on his head and nobody would have noticed.

A few moments later, they arrived at Patti's house. Patti and her friends flowed through the front door and closed it behind them.

Arthur slowly walked up the steps and stopped just inside (outside) the door. Through the large front window he could see colorful streaks of energy running back and forth. Laughter escaped through the keyhole and snaked its way up to his ears. His hands were trembling. He considered walking home and never showing his face at school again. He considered running away to the forest and living like a hobo, eating roots and leaves for the rest of his life. All these thoughts were flashing through his mind when Patti LaVernon opened the door and smiled at him.

"There you are," said Patti.

Arthur's heart fluttered. All his fears were washed away and replaced by newer, happier fears. He tried to say something but all that came out was a hiccup.

"Get in here," said Patti. She grabbed Arthur by the sleeve and dragging him outside (inside).

CHAPTER 10

"It is too easy to die. It should be much harder."
– *Elias Canetti*

****

The world is getting worse. Dim people are procreating at higher rates than bright people.

This is Darwin's loophole: that the fittest would choose not to procreate. Or I should say, that those who are in an ideal mental, social and economic position, would choose not to procreate. That they would rather enjoy their lives than sacrifice them to take care of a living, breathing, pooping, eating, miniature version of themselves.

****

The house was empty. Sheila sat on the edge of her bed and stared at her reflection in the mirror. She barely recognized the fearful creature peering back at her. She sighed and flopped down on the bed. She punched her pillow with both fists. The pillow was hard and heavy. If thrown at a wall, it would leave a hole.

Sheila closed her eyes and felt the future rushing backwards into the present. She felt the memories as they approached from somewhere in the distance and plunged like a needle through her eyes and down into the back of her throat.

Sheila tried to blot out the painful thoughts but her imagination had broken free of its leash. It was running wild, supplying Sheila with a continuous stream of foggy images: angry crowds storming her bedroom, yelling at her and hitting her, tying her up, dragging her to the middle of town and burning her at the stake amid a pile of dry brush, laughing and jeering, spitting at her, waving signs and jumping around like wild animals.

And at the center of the commotion was Mayor Cotton. He was sitting on an elevated throne, smiling and eating a sandwich. He laughed and little bits of lettuce shot out of his mouth. He threw his sandwich at Sheila and a tomato slapped her in the face, sticking momentarily to her cheek before sliding slowly to the ground.

It was all too much for her to take. Why did Mayor Cotton want to kill permaniums? Why couldn't he just leave her in peace? Why did he throw away a perfectly good sandwich?

For the next two hours Sheila attempted, unsuccessfully, to fall asleep. She rolled over and switched sides for the hundredth time. She stuffed the hard pillow in between her knees. Her anxious mumbles echoed and filled the immense silence like a hundred idle engines.

"I've fallen asleep nearly every night for my entire life," she said. "I've had so much practice, you'd think I'd be good at it by now."

She finally drifted off to sleep and in her sleep she mumbled, "Why won't they leave me alone? Why won't they leave me alone?" over and over. Her dreams were filled with angry floating heads, long orange licks of fire, and lots of death.

****

Sheila had once written a short story about fashion. It went something like this:
There once existed a small town where people walked around naked. They were innocent people and they felt no shame.

Then one day a young man invented a material that was intended to cover a person's upper body. He bought a patent and named his invention the "t-shirt."

The t-shirt quickly caught on. It grew in popularity and soon began to fly off the shelves. Yes, people looked very nice walking around in their t-shirts. Nakedness was out, and t-shirts were in.

The young inventor soon became one of the richest men in town. But he was not satisfied with his wealth. After some deliberation, he decided to create multiple lines of t-shirts in order to increase his profits. He sewed large numbers onto the front of every t-shirt. The numbers ranged from 1 to 100. The t-shirts with higher numbers on the front were more expensive. For example, a t-shirt with the number 1 on it cost $5, a t-shirt with the number 5 on it cost $25, and a t-shirt with the number 100 on it, which was very rare, cost $1,000.

A curious thing began to happen. People clambered, cheated, scrimped, and scrounged to get their hands on a t-shirt with a high number sewn on the front.

The inventor's house was soon full of stacks and stacks of money.

By law, homeless people were prohibited

from wearing a t-shirt with a number any higher than a 5 on it. It was very rare to see a woman sporting a t-shirt with a number higher than 50. Some spoiled kids with rich parents had drawers full of t-shirts with 78s, 84s, and even 93s sewn on the front of each one. Every so often you could catch a glimpse of a person wearing a shirt with a 100 on it, but they would never see you.

Eventually people began to realize that t-shirts made them sweaty, itchy and uncomfortable. So they stopped wearing t-shirts and went back to walking around naked.

But then someone invented a line of pants with letters sewn on the rear.

They were very nice pants.

****

The sun was rising as Jim stumbled down the dusty street. The morning fog illuminated his silhouette, much like a flashlight illuminates the body of a fish underwater (if you were, for some reason, to shine a flashlight on a fish underwater).

To a person awaking from a dream and peering out their window, Jim could have been easily mistaken for a glowing angelic emissary sent from the sun on his daily mission to bring the morning rays down to earth, dragging the first glimmers of sunlight in a wispy trail behind him, hunched over and bathed in a soft glow, dripping buckets of sweat as he walked dutifully from one town to the next.

The birds took no notice of this raggedy being from a distant star and continued to screech like monkeys from high atop their wooden perches.

A full day had passed since Jim had departed from his family. He hadn't gotten very far. He had passed through the town of Millington earlier that morning, and was now entering Hoovermont, which was about 25 miles from Turtle Pond, and 95 miles from Paxton. Jim still had a long way to go.

After walking straight through the night, all Jim wanted was to find somewhere to sleep, just for a couple of hours. After that, he'd wake up and hitchhike the rest of the way to Paxton.

If all went according to plan, Jim would be in Paxton by nightfall. There, he would buy as many bottles of Vivacious Vincenzo's Special Shampoo Formula For Men as they would allow him to buy, and would return home to his family the following morning. They wouldn't even notice he had left.

Jim looked up and saw the town sign for Hoovermont. Parked beside the sign was an old yellow Toyota that appeared to be abandoned. The roof was slightly caved in and the yellow paint on the passenger door was badly scratched. There was enough rust on the car to kill a small robot, but it certainly looked comfortable enough to sleep in.

Jim approached the car and tried the rear door handle. The door jerked open with a loud creak. Little flakes of rust rained down on Jim's shoes. Jim climbed into the back seat. It was nice and warm. He immediately felt a sleepy happiness wash over him.

He scanned the interior of the car and noticed a statuette of Jesus Christ standing on the front dashboard, held in place by a single suction cup. The Jesus was smiling an all-knowing, peaceful smile, the one that he and Buddha are so talented at pulling off. Jim felt reassured. He curled up into the fetal position and fell asleep safely under the loving gaze of the dashboard Jesus.

****

There was only one nurse in Turtle Pond. Her name was Rita McClurg. Rita worked alongside Dr. Fern at the little doctor's office on Turtle Pond Road. Rita was responsible for measuring and weighing patients, and giving them their shots, and Dr. Fern was responsible for wearing a long white coat, stroking his mustache, and using long, confusing words.

Dr. Fern's mustache was thick and bushy and it made Karl nervous. Karl was always nervous around people with mustaches, especially people who pet their mustaches like they would a living animal. Karl didn't trust Dr. Fern, even though Dr. Fern had never done anything to make Karl feel this way. A man can live his entire life as a saint, but if he has a mustache, he may as well be Lucifer himself.

Nurse Rita was bright and round, in her early thirties, and had a very sweet disposition that was fitting for a young nurse. She always put on just the right amount of makeup to make herself look like a lovely porcelain doll. Nurse Rita smiled at everyone who came through the door, and knew the name of every child in town.

Nurse Rita was the good cop and Dr. Fern

was the bad cop. They went through their routine over and over again through the course of the each day, with Rita smiling and cooing and Dr. Fern frowning and stroking his mustache. The good cop, bad cop routine is really just a variation on the male, female routine.

When Karl entered Dr. Fern's office, there was no one in the waiting room except for a receptionist who was sitting behind the front desk, delicately painting her fingernails. Karl watched her as she painted her nails alternatingly pink and purple. Karl had never seen her before. She must be new, probably from out of town. After blowing on her nails for a while, she looked up and saw Karl.

"Ah, you must be James," she said.

"Yes, that's me," said Karl.

"Go right in, James," she said. "Nurse Rita is waiting for you."

Karl strolled into the cramped, whitewashed examining room and jumped up on the soft sticky black bed.

"Oh, hello Karl," said Nurse Rita, turning and smiling. "I didn't know you were coming in today."

"Rita," said Karl, "what's a permanium?"

"Oh," Nurse Rita's smile wavered. She closed the door and turned to face Karl.

"Karl, sweetie, where did you hear that word?"

"What, permanium?"

"Yes, that's the one."

"Well, I heard it on the news yesterday morning, and then Mayor Cotton made an announcement about permaniums last night.

Plus there are signs all over town."

"Oh," said Nurse Rita. "Of course."

Karl noticed a worried look in Nurse Rita's eyes.

"Did Reynold Reynoldson do something bad?" asked Karl.

"No Karl, Reynold didn't do anything bad," Rita spoke slowly and softly, her eyes darting uncertainly from Karl's face to various corners of the room. "But I can't answer your question. You'll have to ask your parents when you go home tonight."

"But I already asked my mom and she said she didn't know," Karl was dejected.

Rita sighed and her shoulders slouched forward. She was anxious to get this conversation over with.

"Can you at least give me a hint?" begged Karl.

"A permanium..." Rita thought for a moment, "is someone who is... different from other people."

Karl leaned forward expectantly.

"That's all I can say," said Rita. She walked to the desk and flipped open Karl's file.

"Now," said Rita, "let's take a look at you, young man."

Karl hopped off the bed and opened the door.

"Where are you going?" asked Rita.

"I don't have an appointment," said Karl, and he strolled through (out) the door, leaving Rita staring after him like a confused porcelain doll.

As Karl walked inside (outside) into the sun, a young boy he recognized from the schoolyard was approaching the front door. Karl held the door open for him.

"Hello James," said Karl.

CHAPTER 11

"It's possible to love a human being if you don't know them too well." – *Charles Bukowski*

****

Yes, and it's possible to hate someone you do not know at all, especially if they look like a more popular version of you.

****

Arthur was the life of the party. He was a hit, a star. He had Patti and her friends holding their stomachs, bowled over in childish conniptions, belly laughing with tears in their eyes. And what was Arthur doing that they found so hilarious? He was simply reciting all the books of the Bible.

"Genesis, Exodus, Leviticus, Numbers, Deuteronomy…"

Arthur didn't understand his sudden ascendance to popularity, but he had never been so happy in his life.

"They really like me," he thought.

What Arthur didn't know was that Patti and

her friends were laughing because they thought he was re-enacting the sneezing episode with Mrs. Harrison from the previous morning.

Some of Patti's friends made exaggerated sneezing sounds, shooting flecks of spittle into each other's faces. One boy jumped up on a chair and sneezed on the grandfather clock, covering the glass face with dripping, bubbly sneeze juice. This only sent the group into further hysterics.

Arthur did not wish to bring the festivities to a halt, so he continued standing in the corner and reciting the books of the Bible, starting over at Genesis every time he reached Revelations.

Arthur was confused. He was in heaven. Heaven was confusing.

Arthur didn't know it at the time, but before he left Patti LaVernon's house, something would happen to him that would change his life forever.

****

Someone was tapping on the window. Jim opened his eyes to see a field of yellow fluffy fuzz. He was lying in the fetal position in the back seat of the rusted yellow Toyota, his head leaning awkwardly up against the door, and his face squashed against the back of the front seat.

A man in a plain white t-shirt was tapping his finger on the rear window. Jim's joints popped and clicked as he pulled himself up and opened the door.

"Hello," Jim greeted the man.

"Hi," said the man. A soft carpet of casual stubble covered his relaxed jaw line. His eyes, strangely bright, were only made brighter in contrast to the dark half moons looming beneath them.

"Did you have a good sleep?" asked the man.

"Yes, thank you," said Jim.

"That's good," said the man. "And did you have any dreams?"

"No," said Jim, "not that I can remember." He rubbed his chin thoughtfully. "Well, maybe one or two."

The man nodded. He seemed to be waiting for something. Jim stared with blurry eyes at the man's brown shoes, and absentmindedly rubbed the yellow fabric of the car seat with his hand.

"This is my car," said the man.

"Oh," Jim snapped out of his daze. "I'm terribly sorry." Jim struggled to pull himself out of the back seat. He stood up and faced the man. Slightly embarrassed and not knowing what to say, Jim turned and walked sheepishly away down the sidewalk.

"Hey, do you need a ride somewhere?" the man called after him.

"I'm trying to get to Paxton," Jim called back. After a pause he added, "It's very important I get there by tonight."

The man thought for a moment.

"Alright," he said, "I can take you halfway."

Jim ran back to the car and jumped in the passenger seat. As the car sputtered down the road, Jim's eyes fell on the dashboard Jesus. The wobbling Jesus smiled lovingly at him, as if he understood the pain Jim was feeling in his stiffened joints and shrunken stomach. Jim looked out the window and yawned. After ten minutes or so, Jim broke the silence.

"Are you a Christian or something?" he asked the man.

The man had seen Jim eying the dashboard Jesus.

"Well that's a tough question," he said. "I believe in kindness. I know that much for certain." The man's eyes brightened. "And that's what Jesus believed in too, kindness," he continued. "So I guess that kinda means I believe in Jesus." The man looked over to find that Jim had fallen asleep. He finished his thought quietly, so as not to wake Jim.

"And if you believe in kindness then I guess I believe in you too."

****

The only time Jim had ever stepped foot inside a church was five years ago, on Christmas Eve. All he remembered from that night was singing sad-sounding songs and listening to a deathly old man talk about the Messiah.

Halfway through the service, Jim had scanned the faces around him to find that half the people were sleeping.

"Some birthday party this is," Jim muttered under his breath.

Sheila overheard him and jabbed a sharp elbow into his ribs.

For the rest of the service Jim held a singular, vivid vision in his head. It was the vision of Jesus Christ himself wearing a colorful party hat, sitting on the edge of the stage with his chin resting in the palms of his hands, bored out of his mind at his own birthday party.

****

The only time Jim had ever spoken with a priest was two years ago, while sitting in a dingy diner on lunch break. Jim was sitting alone in a corner booth and the priest walked through (in) the front door of the diner and sat down across from him. His eyes were calm and alert, and he held his chin angled slightly downwards as he walked.

The priest was going through a period of intense doubt in his faith and was taking time off from the church to wander the countryside and rediscover the universe.

The priest looked Jim in the eye, and with a tinge of desperation in his soft voice, began unloading his thoughts onto a complete stranger. Here is what he said:

"There is an entire half of Christianity, and all organized religion, that I do not understand. I understand the part about kindness and compassion and loving your neighbour. That's all great. But I don't understand how a person can be expected to love God, or why so much importance is placed upon this fundamentally confusing principle.

"I mean, I don't even know the guy. I'd love to know him. I'd love to meet him or even speak to him just once. I know who he supposedly is. I love the *idea* of him. I love what he stands for, love and mercy and creativity and forgiveness and all that. I really do. But is loving what a person stands for the same as loving a person?" The priest paused for a moment and observed the slightly confused look on Jim's face.

"Here, maybe I'd better give you an example," he said. "Imagine I describe a person to you. You don't know this person and you've never met them. I tell you all about their personality, their values, their likes and dislikes. I even tell you that this person, who you don't know, loves you very much. After that, I show you some beautiful sculptures and paintings that this person has supposedly made, though there is no concrete proof of his authorship. Then I ask you to love this person who you've never met or spoken to, but whom I've described to you in great detail, and who I've assured you exists. What would you say?"

Jim chewed his sandwich and looked blankly at the priest.

"I don't know," Jim mumbled.

"Well," the priest cut back in, "I'd probably say that that's impossible for me to do. I'd say that this person sounds very nice, but I don't even know whether they exist or not, whether they're real or imaginary. I simply cannot whole-heartedly love a being that I've never met, who I don't really *know*. The idea of doing so seems a bit naïve to me. However, I *can* imagine loving this person if I were given the opportunity to actually meet them and to get to know them. It would be easy to love such a person, yes, if he really existed.

"I can love a person's work. I can love a piece of art. I can love nature. I can love music. I can even love other people sometimes. But I find it an impossible task to love a being whose existence I doubt on a day-to-day basis.

"Perhaps my idea of love is flawed from the start," the priest sighed heavily. "Perhaps love is meant to be like a rollercoaster. 'I love you today. I may not love you tomorrow. But two days from now, I'll probably love you again.' Perhaps it cannot be any other way."

With that, the priest stood up, thanked Jim, and strolled inside (outside), feeling slightly better about the universe.

CHAPTER 12

"Man is a creature that can get accustomed to anything, and I think that is the best definition of him." – *Fyodor Dostoevsky*

****

"I believe the best definition of man is the ungrateful biped." – *Fyodor Dostoevsky*

****

While on his way to visit Luigi, the town barber, Karl walked past a pair of twenty-something-year-old kids who were fondling each other on the side of Turtle Pond Road. They were much too old to be kissing in public, but chose to do so anyway, much to the dismay of everyone around them.

Karl was reminded of something his grandfather used to say, before he passed away: "Public displays of affection deserve to be stared at until the perpetrators become uncomfortable and cease their stupidity."

Karl stopped and peered up at the couple, just like his grandfather would have wanted him to.

"Excuse me," said Karl. "Can either one of you tell me what a permanium is?"

The couple halted their parasitic lip-locking and looked down at Karl with disdain and annoyance. The boy's lips were red with lipstick that had jumped from the girl's lips to his.

"Of course we know what a permanium is," the boy spit his words at Karl.

"Oh good! Great!" Karl was excited. "So what is it? What's a permanium?"

The kids simultaneously sneered.

"It's your mother!" the girl blurted out.

The couple doubled over in laughter. After a few moments they resumed their awkward, creepy, leech-like embrace, and pretended that Karl wasn't there.

Karl walked away with his shoulders slightly slumped.

"Well that wasn't helpful at all," said Karl.

****

Here is yet another meaningless sidenote: Last week was that boy's 20th birthday. He had celebrated his birthday by eating a slab of plain vanilla cake on a Styrofoam plate. His father and brother were there too. They had all eaten their cake in silence. The boy did not have a mother. She probably died or ran away or got divorced and remarried or something.

After finishing their cake, the father had handed the boy a birthday card. Inside the card the boy's father had written these words:

"Cheers son, to another 60 years of being alive, to another 50 years of being aware, to another 40 years of having a sex drive, to another 30 years of having good eyesight, to another 20 years of having a full head of hair, to another 10 years of having fun.
Love Always,
Dad."

****

Karl didn't take the rude comment about his mother personally, but it reminded him of the first time somebody had made a joke about his mother. In grade one, Karl's friend Wally told Karl that his mother looked like a man. Some other kids overheard this comment and laughed. Karl ran away crying.

As time went by, Karl got used to kids making jokes about his mother. We all get used to it. By the time a child reaches grade three, mother jokes are about as shocking as seeing the sun rise each morning.

We just get used to things, I guess.

We just get used to things.

****

If you spent a year living on a moving rollercoaster, would the experience eventually become comparable to taking a stroll down the street?

Probably.

You'd get used to it. And soon you'd get so used to it that you wouldn't want to get *off* the rollercoaster.

The human body has an amazing ability to adapt to its environment.

We just get used to things.

****

Maybe pain never goes away. Maybe we just get used to it.

CHAPTER 13

"To avoid criticism, do nothing, say nothing, and be nothing." – *Elbert Hubbard*

****

It's true, Patti LaVernon's parents were both blind as bats. When Patti had friends over and didn't want her parents to know, they would all tiptoe around the house, careful not to cough or sneeze or knock anything over. Patti could get away with virtually anything, as long as she did it silently.

On one occasion when Patti's parents grounded her, Patti took revenge by inviting 20 friends over to her house after her parents had gone to bed. Overcome with rebellious glee, Patti and her friends danced circles around her sleeping parents, on their tiptoes of course. They waved strange fruits and vegetables in the air above Patti's parents, and then watched with pleasure as their noses twitched and their faces washed over with sleepy confusion.

The game had come to an abrupt end when one boy, taking the joke too far, decided to pull down his pants and fart directly into Patti's father's face. It was the same boy who, months later, would sneeze on Patti's grandfather clock.

****

"If only I could fit twelve hours rest into six hours sleep," Sheila mumbled to herself as she stumbled down Turtle Pond Road. She felt slightly better after her nap. The fear had evaporated somewhere behind her eyelids. Perhaps she had passed the fear off to the people in her dreams.

Sheila took a deep breath and exhaled. It felt good to be inside (outside). She chuckled as she thought about how unnecessarily scared she had been just a few hours ago. Now that she was inside (outside) breathing fresh air, she could see that there was nothing to be worried about.

Sheila strolled leisurely down the sidewalk. She closed her eyes and let her body relax. When she opened her eyes, a small group of people had emerged from around the corner and was walking in her direction.

A group of geese is a gaggle, a group of lions is a pride, a group of sheep is a herd, but what is the special word that describes a group of humans? A business? A crowd? A spectacle? A corporation? A gang? Sartre would say, "hell."

Sheila immediately tensed up. Her eyes darted across the street, searching for an escape. It was too late. The people were upon her.

The group stopped just two feet in front of Sheila. A tall bearded man stepped forward and held up his right hand. He appeared to be the leader of the gang.

"Alright guys," said the leader. "You know what to do."

Sheila figured that these people must have somehow found out her secret. She closed her eyes and prepared for the worst. She waited for the fists to start raining down on her. But they never came.

Instead, a woman's voice called out, "Three cheers for permaniums!"

"Hip! Hip! Hooray!" the voices yelled in unison.

Sheila peeked up at the group. She looked at the faces in the group and saw that they were all smiling. Sheila looked harder and was sure she saw something sinister behind their smiles, an angry glint behind their eyes.

"Hip! Hip! Hooray!"

The loud voices sent shivers down Sheila's spine. Her body shook with every shout. The yelling people gestured at her, beckoning her to fall in step and join their cause. They wanted her to help them show support for permaniums. Meanwhile, they were oblivious to the fact that they were staring a permanium in the face and scaring the daylights out of her.

"Hip! Hip! Hooray!"

Sheila took off running. She sprinted through a narrow alley and emerged onto a small street where a parade was in progress.

Bunches of people streamed down the street, some adorned in bright costumes, some holding hands and singing, some waving permanium-themed banners and homemade signs. The scene somehow reminded Sheila of a Nazi demonstration she had once seen on TV.

Sheila watched as a man wearing face paint and dressed as a clown walked past her. The clown noticed Sheila and gestured for her to join the parade. Sheila drew back into the alleyway.

"Aren't permaniums great?" the clown yelled at her. He opened his mouth wide and laughed.

Sheila trembled and hid her face with her hand. Where did all these people come from? Where were they all headed? Probably to the centre of town to organize search parties to hunt down all the permaniums and exterminate them.

Sheila was breathing fast, her heart beating against her ribs. She was positive that everyone in the parade somehow knew her secret, and would be coming to get her soon.

No longer able to contain her terror, Sheila let out a nervous, muffled scream. A group of people wearing brightly coloured bird feathers stopped walking and stared at her.

"Who is that?" Sheila heard one of them say. The feathered people strained to see Sheila's face.

Sheila spun on her heels and sprinted all the way home. She hurried outside (inside), flung the door closed behind her, and collapsed on the floor. She reached up and locked the deadbolt. It clicked into place with the finality of a death sentence.

Sheila began to sob quietly there on the floor. Gasping and crying, she made up her mind that she could not go on living like this. Something had to change.

****

Sheila once wrote a short story that debated whether or not the story was enjoyable. The story was titled, "Harold's Taxi." The characters in the story argued over the merit of the story and often referred to themselves by name.

One character named Riley declared that, "Riley is an altogether slimy and underhanded man who does not deserve to lick the dirt off my shoes."

Another character named Melody observed that, "Melody is rather bland and tends to drag down the narrative atmosphere. She is simply not very intelligent."

A rather amiable character named Henry stated that, "It was such a shame when Henry got run over by a bus."

He was then run over by a bus.

A cute little girl named Yolanda piped up and said, "I thought it was funny!"

Harold the artist quickly scoffed at her, saying, "You imbecile child! It was the opposite of funny. It was a truly dreadful story! Not much of a story at all really. Its only saving grace was that wonderfully insightful artist character, Harold, I believe his name was. I only wish he played a bigger role."

Harold then hailed a taxi and drove away, leaving the rest of the characters standing in a cloud of dust and exhaust fumes.

Yolanda began to cry.

"Don't worry, honey," Melody comforted her. "Remember, at the end of the story Harold's taxi drove off a cliff."

CHAPTER 14

"Start a huge, foolish project, like Noah. It makes absolutely no difference what people think of you." – *Rumi*

****

This part isn't funny, so feel free to skip ahead: It's a miracle that we get out of bed each day, that we find the strength to rise from our chair after dinner instead of letting our head fall forward into our half-eaten bowl of soup. And even though we know that nothing is important, even though we know that everything is meaningless, we are still obligated to act. And that is what we do. We act. We act our hearts out, with forced smiles, sad songs and make-believe relationships we know are doomed to fail from the start. But still we go through the motions for the sake of the invisible audience.

Everything we do, in some way, is to

improve the present moment. Everything we do aims to minimize our future pain, because all future moments will soon become the present moment, and the last thing we want to feel in the present is pain.

So we must act, for the sake of this moment and the next. We must pretend that life is serious, even when we want to burst out laughing. We must pretend that things are important, even when we know they're not.

****

"Of course I know what a permanium is," said Luigi Labriola.

He laughed and stroked his mustache with his left hand. The scissors in his right hand moved with lightning fast precision around the man's head seated on the elevated chair in front of him.

Luigi Labriola had been cutting hair and shaving faces in Turtle Pond for nearly 25 years. The walls of Luigi's barbershop were covered with detailed sketches of the heads of every person in Turtle Pond, including measurements of hair length, location of hairline, and thickness of hair. Each sketch was drawn from four different angles: front, top, back and side. Everyone in town agreed that Luigi gave perfect haircuts.

But Luigi hadn't always been so successful. Before he became Luigi Labriola, his name had been Felix Johnson. And before Luigi Labriola had opened up "Luigi's Italian Barber Shop", Felix Johnson had opened a place called "Turtle Pond Hair Cuts," which had gone out of business after only two weeks. Nobody had come to get their hair cut.

So Felix Johnson had gone back to the drawing board. He changed his name to Luigi Labriola. He straightened his curly red hair. He dyed it jet black and greased it flat against his head. He grew a mustache, dyed it jet black too, and greased it against his upper lip.

He tore down the old "Turtle Pond Hair Cuts" sign and put up a new sign that read "Luigi's Italian Barber Shop" in sleek black italics. This seemed to lend Luigi some credibility as a legitimate barber.

People began to trickle in and soon word had spread around town that Luigi the Italian Barber was indeed an excellent barber.

Nobody ever caught on that Luigi Labriola the Italian barber was actually Felix Johnson the redheaded haircutter. Stereotypes are always more credible because of their utter simplicity and predictability, and because they connect with all the junk swirling around in the backs of our heads.

"So what is it then?" Karl peered up at Luigi expectantly.

Luigi pretended to concentrate hard as he delicately snipped the little hairs around the man's ears. He was stalling for time.

"Well, a permanium is –"

"Yow!" yelled the man, as Luigi clipped the back of his ear.

"Mama mia!" said Luigi.

He had clipped the man's ear intentionally to buy more time to think of an answer.

"A permanium," he said to Karl with an air of authority, "is a person who can see the future."

"Hmm," said Karl. "So a permanium is kind of like a fortune teller?"

"Kind of," said Luigi. "But permaniums can actually see the future, while fortune tellers cannot. Fortune tellers are fake permaniums."

Karl took a notepad out of his back pocket and wrote this down.

"Isn't that right?" Luigi nudged the man sitting in front of him.

"That's right," said the man. The man actually thought that a permanium was a person who was unable to grow eyebrows, but he was too frightened to disagree with Luigi, the man who was wielding a pair of scissors only inches away from his head.

Karl thanked Luigi and walked inside (outside). He was fairly certain that Luigi was wrong about what a permanium was, but every bit of information helped.

****

Jim was hungry. He was also lonely. His loneliness made his hunger worse. He was only on the second day of his journey, and already he was missing his family.

Jim was presently in the town of Hamsterville, 68 miles from his house in Turtle Pond and 52 miles from Vivacious Vincenzo's Shampoo Emporium in Paxton.

The man in the yellow Toyota had said farewell to Jim in the center of Hamsterville, before taking off in the direction they had come from. Shortly after the man drove away, Jim realized that his wallet was no longer in his pocket. It must have fallen out in the man's car, and now he had no way of getting it back. Jim emptied the contents of his pockets to find that his personal possessions now amounted to a paper clip, a sizeable wad of lint, and the key to his house in Turtle Pond.

Jim squinted his eyes and wiped the sweat from his brow. It was mid-day and the sun was beating down from the sky like a giant sizzling egg yolk. The clouds looked like fluffy, butter-soaked pieces of toast. The earth smoldered like a frying pan, coated in bubbling oil. It was so hot even the birds refused to sing.

Jim walked down the main street of Hamsterville and saw a young freckle-faced boy strolling towards him, munching on a glowing red apple the size of a grapefruit. Jim's head swiveled as they passed, his hungry eyes burning a hole through the boy's giant apple.

The boy didn't notice Jim, and took another chomp out of the side of his apple. A torrent of juice splashed out of the gaping hole in the apple and landed in the gutter where it formed a small river and flowed down into the sewer. Jim stared in amazement at the river of apple juice. He looked longingly down the street after the freckle-faced boy.

A pudgy lady with a mustard-stained sweater followed shortly after the boy, gnawing on a caveman-sized chicken wing. The grease on her lips and cheeks and chin glistened in the egg yolk sun. Jim's gaze was transfixed on the chicken wing being held tightly in her meaty fist.

The pudgy lady's body odor overpowered the scent from the succulent chicken. She left an aroma in her wake that reminded Jim of old cheddar cheese.

Jim's mouth was full of saliva. It overflowed and leaked down, filling in the cracks and holes in the sidewalk, merging with the still raging apple juice river. Jim licked his parched lips, and his stomach grumbled violent obscenities.

Jim's least favorite smell in the world was a fat person's body odor, but he was so starving mad with hunger that this pudgy lady's cheddar cheese scent was enough to make him want to lick her armpits.

This should give you an idea of how hungry Jim was.

****

Jim gazed longingly at the retreating back of the pudgy greasy-faced lady. He considered running past her and snatching the chicken from her hands in full sprint. She'd never be able to catch him. Before Jim could develop this plan any further, the pudgy lady tossed the bone over her shoulder and continued waddling down the street.

Jim swooped down on his greasy prize like a vulture. He sat on the curb and delicately picked at the bone with his fingers, tossing microscopic bits of chicken into his mouth, one after another. When the bone was picked clean, Jim sucked the fat and cartilage off the ends and dropped it back into the gutter.

A man wearing a green apron emerged from the grocery store behind Jim and told him to get lost or else he'd call the cops. Jim picked himself up from the curb and resumed walking in the direction of Paxton.

CHAPTER 15

"Probably the closest things to perfection are the huge absolutely empty holes that astronomers have recently discovered in space. If there's nothing there, how can anything go wrong?" – *Richard Brautigan*

****

Arthur sat quietly at Patti's kitchen table feeling lost, helpless and dumb. Patti and her friends were discussing fashion and music and celebrities and other things that Arthur knew nothing about.

The conversation presently shifted to sports, which didn't help Arthur at all. He knew even less about sports than he knew about fashion.

One of Patti's friends was arguing loudly, saying that women were more skilled at basketball than men. Arthur had never seen a women's basketball game, but he had always assumed that female basketball players were required to wear high-heeled shoes on the court.

To prove her point, the girl asked Arthur to toss her a ceramic teapot that was sitting on the kitchen table. She would catch it no problem, she said. That's how confident she was in her skilled, steady, female hands.

Arthur picked up the teapot and threw it to her. It bounced off her fingertips and crashed to the floor, breaking into hundreds of tiny, delicate, unrepairable pieces. The girl put her hands over her mouth and gasped. Patti spun and glared at Arthur.

"Why'd you do that?" she shrieked.

Arthur shrank down in his chair and said nothing. Patti looked so angry that for a moment Arthur thought she was going to hit him. Instead, Patti groaned and tears began to well up in her eyes.

"My parents are going to kill me," she said.

Arthur hugged his knees and wished he could disappear. The room was full of silent accusations. Nobody moved. Then one of the girls jumped up from her chair.

"My parents have an extra teapot they never use," she said. "You can put it on your table and your parents will never know the difference... because they're blind," she added unnecessarily.

Patti thought for a moment and took an angry swipe at her eyes.

"Alright," she said to the girl. "Go get it. Hurry up!"

The girl took off running, happy to be able to do a favor for Patti LaVernon, the coolest girl in school.

Patti was slightly embarrassed for having cried in front of her friends over a broken teapot. She turned to Arthur and her embarrassment quickly turned into anger.

"I'm still mad at you," she said, through

clenched teeth.

"But it wasn't my fault," Arthur squeaked.

"Yes," said Patti, "it *was* your fault. You're the one who threw it, weren't you?"

"Yes, but-" Arthur wanted so desperately for Patti to like him again. He tried to think of a way to make it up to her.

"At least your parents are blind," said Arthur. "They'll never even know we broke their teapot."

"*You* broke their teapot," said Patti. "*You* broke it." She turned her back on him.

It occurred to Arthur that perhaps he should change the subject. It never occurred to him that the best thing to do would be to stop talking.

"Isn't it strange," said Arthur, "that both of your parents are blind, yet you have perfect 20/20 vision?"

Patti spun back to face Arthur.

"I... I mean," he stammered, trying desperately to say the right thing. "Did you ever think that maybe you were adopted?"

Patti's face darkened and Arthur could see that he had touched a sore spot. Patti's eyes flashed with anger.

"I am *not* adopted!" yelled Patti. She shoved Arthur hard. Arthur's chair wobbled and he flailed his arms wildly, trying to regain his balance.

As Arthur fell, two things happened. First, he sneezed in mid-air, and second, he banged his head off the corner of the kitchen table. Arthur's body went limp, and as he slid to the floor, his world went black.

****

Arthur was having a dream in which Patti LaVernon hovered over him like an angel. She had cashmere wings and a golden halo and beautiful silver pupils. On her face was a look of loving concern. Her lips were moving, but Arthur couldn't hear anything coming out of them.

"Mmmm," Arthur mumbled. "Patti... you... you have really nice lips... And... when you talk... your lips do really nice things."

The angel Patti LaVernon frowned and slapped Arthur across the face, but not too hard. It was a loving, angelic slap, the kind of slap only a woman or child or sensitive man with soft hands is capable of.

Arthur realized he was not dreaming. The angels in his dreams never slapped him.

"Are you okay?" asked Patti.

Arthur could hear her now. The slap had cleared his ears.

"Where am I?" asked Arthur. His head was pounding just above his left temple. He felt dazed, stunned, helpless, like he had just awoken from a hazy dream to find himself stuck in an even hazier dream. All he could think about was how much he enjoyed eggs and toast for breakfast.

Arthur peered up at the faces all around him. He remembered who Patti was, but he could not figure out who all the other people were, though he had a vague feeling he had seen them before.

Arthur tried to remember how he came to be laying on the floor in this strange kitchen.

The last thing he remembered was sneezing and falling out of a chair. He tried to think of his own name but could not recall it.

Arthur's eyes widened in horror. Oh no! It had finally happened...

****

What Arthur didn't realize, and what nobody told him, was that when he banged his head off the table he had sustained a serious concussion. Common symptoms of a concussion are headache, dizziness, and temporary memory loss.

****

Arthur sat at Patti's kitchen table in a daze. His eyes were glazed over like delicious eyeball-shaped donuts.

"Did somebody break something?" He pointed at the broken pieces of teapot on the floor. Nobody responded. Arthur appeared to be okay, so everybody was ignoring him again. Arthur looked around the room from face to face, still trying to figure out who these strange people were.

Without realizing what he was doing, Arthur began mumbling to himself.

"Genesis... Genesis... Genisis..." A confused look flashed across his face. "Genesis... Genisis... Genesis... Exodus... Exodus..." Arthur recognized the words that were coming out of his mouth. He knew that many more words were supposed to follow them. "Genesis... Genesis... Exodus... Exodus... Exodus..."

Arthur felt instinctively that something was terribly wrong. He didn't know where he was, he didn't know who the people around him were, he couldn't remember what came after "Genesis, Exodus," he couldn't even remember his own name!

Arthur felt like crying, but he could not remember whether crying was a good thing or a bad thing, so he was unsure if crying would be appropriate in this situation.

Arthur began to panic. He felt trapped inside. He could not do anything if he did not know the answers to these simple questions: Who am I? Where am I? Who are these people? Why am I here? These unanswered questions began to hold him hostage. They strapped him down and wouldn't let him move. He was neither happy nor sad. He knew that he wouldn't be able to truly feel anything until he answered these questions.

Arthur sprang to his feet, knocked his chair over with a clatter, and ran inside (outside).

Though Arthur did not know it at the time, he would never see Patti LaVernon or any of her friends again.

CHAPTER 16

"Who are my brothers?" – *Jesus Christ*

****

Karl strolled through the doors of Turtle Pond Church to find it empty except for a fat lady praying. The fat lady was kneeling down in the front pew, hands folded and face raised toward heaven. Her chin jiggled peacefully as she projected her fat voice into the holy silence.

Karl was sure there was something symbolic about this fat praying lady, but couldn't put his finger on what it was. The whole scene struck him as odd.

Karl cleared his throat loud enough for the lady to hear. She began praying louder, with more passion. Her chin jiggled rhythmically, hypnotically. Karl cleared his throat again, louder this time. The lady turned and looked at Karl, pretending to be surprised.

"Oh," she said, struggling to her feet. "I didn't hear you there."

Karl was amazed at her incredible girth. "I'm sorry to interrupt you," he said.

"Oh, that's okay," said the fat lady. "The big man upstairs can wait." She pointed toward the high ceiling with a chubby finger. "I can talk to him anytime."

"What do you mean?" asked Karl.

The fat lady was now standing directly in front of him. She smelled like feet, and Karl struggled to keep from scrunching his nose. He breathed through his mouth instead.

"I mean I can talk to God anytime," said the fat lady. "I just have to call on him and he'll be there for me."

"You mean you can actually talk to God?" asked Karl.

"Well of course, child." The fat lady softly

snorted. "If I ever need help with anything I just ask him and he helps me out."

Karl was shocked. Who was this fat lady who had frequent conversations with God?

"Can I talk to God too?" asked Karl. "Can you teach me how?"

"Of course," said the fat lady. "All you have to do is talk and God will listen."

"I don't get it," said Karl. "How do I know that he's listening?"

"You just have to have faith," said the fat lady.

"Does he ever talk back to you?" asked Karl. "I mean, can you hear him or does he just listen?"

"Oh, you can hear him alright," said the fat lady. "You just have to listen hard enough. God works in mysterious ways, you know."

"What does that mean?" asked Karl, "That God works in mysterious ways..."

"Well, maybe God is walking right beside you and helping you out and you don't even know it," said the fat lady. "Maybe God's ways are so subtle and mysterious that you don't even notice him working." The fat lady smiled at Karl.

"Hmm," said Karl. "I'm not sure I understand."

"What don't you understand child? It's as simple as night and day."

"Well, I don't understand how God helps us," said Karl. "Is he a real person? Does he reach down to us from the sky?" Karl paused. "I guess I just need an example," he said.

"Okay," said the fat lady. "An example... Hmmm... Well, let's say your grandfather is dying of cancer. God can make it so that your grandfather doesn't feel too much pain when he dies. He can reduce the pain so your grandfather can die peacefully."

"Really?" said Karl.

"Yes, really," said the fat lady. "One time, a friend of mine got into a terrible car accident and broke her spine. She was completely paralyzed. She couldn't move or talk or laugh or feed herself. Her brain was all messed up in the crash too. She's what you would call a *vegetable*. So I went to see her at the hospital and I prayed to God that he would let her die quickly and peacefully. And sure enough, she died the very next day."

"Huh," said Karl.

"You see," said the fat lady, "all it takes is a little faith."

"What does that mean?" asked Karl. "Faith."

"It means trusting in God even when it seems like he's not there. It means believing that God has a plan for your life, that he loves you very much and would never do anything to harm you."

Karl had a momentary flashback to when a young girl in his class gave a speech about all the poor, starving children who were dying in Africa.

"So what about the people who don't ask for God's help?" asked Karl. "God doesn't help them?"

The lady laughed again. "You *do* ask a lot of questions, don't you?"

"I guess faith just confuses me a little," said Karl.

"It's like this," said the fat lady. "If God asks

you to do something, you just do it. If he asks you to feed the poor, you feed the poor. If he asks you to quit your job, you quit your job. If he asks you to slam your head against a wall, you slam your head against a wall, and you do it with joy in your heart. You don't ask questions."

"Why would God ask you to slam your head against a wall?" asked Karl.

The fat lady thought for a moment. "I guess you're right... He probably wouldn't ask you to do that... But you can never be sure... Like I said, God works in mysterious ways." The fat lady winked at Karl.

None of this made any sense to Karl. He was beginning to think that the fat lady might be insane. Nevertheless, his curiosity overruled his confusion and he persisted.

"But how do you know that God is talking to you, and you're not just talking to yourself?"

"It all comes back to faith," said the fat lady, matter-of-factly. She smiled knowingly, showing that she understood completely what was going on in Karl's head. "You just have to believe. The only way to find out is to be obedient to that voice. God is all around us, you know," said the fat lady. "You just have to open your eyes."

Karl felt dizzy and light-headed, as though he had just slammed his head against a wall.

"I don't know," said Karl. "I get the feeling that if God were still at work in the world today, he sure as hell wouldn't come anywhere near North America."

****

"One more question," said Karl as he pulled his notepad out of his back pocket. "Do you know what a permanium is?"

"Oh, of course," said the fat lady. "A permanium is one of those people at the circus who eats fire."

****

People who smile knowingly usually don't know.

****

As Karl walked back through the church doors, he bumped right into his brother Arthur, who was entering the church. Arthur appeared to be drunk. He was stumbling back and forth and tripping over his own feet. As Arthur staggered past Karl, he bumped into his shoulder.

"Sorry," Arthur mumbled and kept on walking.

"Hey Arthur," Karl called after his brother.

Arthur turned and gave Karl an intensely odd look, the kind of look you would give a stranger if they proposed marriage to you while waiting in line at the hardware store.

Arthur had no idea who Karl was. His concussion had scrambled that part of his brain.

****

Arthur entered the church and saw the fat lady praying. He sneezed five times and the fat lady began praying louder. Arthur sneezed again. His sneezes echoed off the walls and disappeared into the dark, cavernous shadows.

"Oh, God bless you child," said the fat lady, turning to face Arthur with a surprised look on her face.

A caped figure suddenly emerged from the shadows. It was a man dressed in black, wearing a crimson-red cape.

The caped man ran up to the fat lady and yelled at the top of his lungs.

"God bless you, indeed! May the angels of God protect this boy from catching a cold! Aha!" The man leaped up onto the nearest pew. "If there were any man whose steps were to be carefully watched by the angels of God, surely it would have been Mozart. If there were any man who would be granted a long life of 90 or 100 years, *surely* it would have been Mozart. Yet Mozart died at age 35. Chopin at 39. Bizet at 36. Goldberg at 29. Gershwin at 38. Schubert at 31 (see appendix).

"Is this not enough proof for you that God favors no man? Where was God while young Mozart was on his deathbed? While we are on this earth, God neither gives life nor takes it away, neither blesses nor curses. But each man is a blessing and a curse unto himself.

"If there is not a God, there should be. And if there is a God, it should be plain to all of us that he is no longer paying attention. He is not reaching down and rewarding some of us for doing good, while punishing others for doing evil.

"How do you explain away all of the evil men who profit enormously, and all of the virtuous, principled men who suffer through life? It cannot be that God arbitrarily chooses to dole out rewards and punishments to some people, on some days, in some cases. And no, the notion of 'character building,' or God's desire for us to build character through pain, is not enough to justify the suffering of an honest man.

"To say that God has blessed you is an insult to God's judgment. To say, after achieving success, that God wanted you to succeed is an insult to all of mankind. It is an insult to the nameless, starving child who prays daily for food yet never receives it. It is an insult to the terminally ill and the diseased who pray for mercy yet still die young and alone. It is an insult to every person who is not you.

"The great Russian author, Ivan Turgenev once said, and I paraphrase, 'The tiny bit of space I occupy is so minute in comparison with the rest of the universe, where I am not and which is not concerned with me; and the period of time in which it is my lot to live is so infinitesimal compared with the eternity in which I have not been and shall not be... And yet here, in this atom which is myself, in this mathematical point, blood circulates, the brain operates and aspires to something too... What a monstrous business! What futility!'

"Perhaps God created us and gave us all the tools we need to be good and kind and loving, and then placed us in a universe that operates on the principle of compensation, where a person is intrinsically rewarded in some way for making good choices, and is intrinsically punished in some way for making bad ones. Maybe the universe adds to us and takes away from us based on the choices we make using our own free will. And I am not referring to the idea of outward, immediately manifested 'karma,' but to the changes that occur within a person's being and accumulate over time to shape one's character.

"The great Marquis de Sade once said of a religiously ignorant girl, 'If those maxims have been carefully concealed from her, she can't be unhappy because of it, for if they are true, the Supreme Being is too just to punish her for her ignorance, and they are false, what need is there to tell her about them?'

"Now tell me, dear fat lady, what justice is there to be found in eternal fire?" The caped man disappeared into the shadows just as quickly as he had emerged.

Arthur wondered if the man was real, or if it had all been a hallucination.

"Genesis, Exodus..." he mumbled.

****

If something saddens you, it saddens God also. If something makes you happy, it makes God happy too. Overall, God couldn't agree with you more.

CHAPTER 17

"People are fond of their children, all right, but if someone said he was fond of God, wouldn't that be blasphemy?" – *Halldor Laxness*

****

To an outsider passing through, small towns appear utterly uneventful. Jim had been walking through small town after small town for the entire day, and the most exciting thing he had encountered was a delirious homeless man.

"You have what it takes!" the homeless man yelled. His eyes were bright, but there was nothing behind them. "Yes! I believe in you!" Apparently the man had gone insane in a very positive direction.

"Thank you, sir," Jim replied and continued walking.

The homeless man stared after him. "I approve, I approve, I approve." The man nodded his head vigorously up and down. "The *universe* approves."

Jim's heels were blistered but he was too tired to feel pain. He rubbed his face and felt a rough layer of stubble. He wasn't used to having facial hair, and enjoyed the feel of the short, sharp whiskers against his fingers. He liked the sound the whiskers made when he stroked his jaw against the grain. It sounded like a comb trying to slice through a carrot.

Jim had grown out his facial hair only once before. After returning from his honeymoon, he'd let loose and grown a thick mustache that curled up at the tips. His mustache was always smiling, even when he wasn't. Jim's mustache experiment had been short-lived, as he'd been forced to shave his face after Sheila accused his mustache of ruining Christmas.

Jim flopped down on a hard wooden bench and looked around. He scanned the storefronts along the street and noticed a sign on the sidewalk that read, "Mama Jo's All-Day Breakfast." Below that, written in white chalk, were the words, "Business Conference Tonight. Closed to the Public. Sorry for the inconvenience." Below that was a painted picture of a large menacing woman with hamhock forearms and the brow of a Neanderthal. Written in pretty pink cursive on her apron was the title, "Mama Jo."

Jim's stomach growled like a wild jaguar. His intestines wrote vigorous love poems and sent them up his esophagus to his rear molars, which were utterly lacking in emotional empathy and robotically chewed the poems to pieces. Jim's ribs struck up a drumbeat on his heart. His liver opened its wormy mouth.

"Go to Mama Jo's," it screamed at Jim.

"Okay," said Jim.

****

There is only one way, *only* one way, to describe the interior of Mama Jo's: it looked like it had been decorated by a band of drunken ballerinas, delicately prancing around, placing random trinkets on rotting shelves, sprinkling handfuls of dust in the air like rice at a wedding, and hanging crooked pictures atop nails which they had spontaneously whacked into the wall using lovely pink hammers that matched their leotards.

Jim limped through (in) the front door, smiled at the hostess and mumbled, "Sorry I'm late." For added effect, he thrust out his hand and enthusiastically pumped the hostess' limp hand up and down.

Jim glided through the crowd of middle-aged whites and headed straight for the buffet line. With his grey suit, open collar and two-day stubble, Jim looked as though he'd been busy crunching numbers and absorbing important business-related material all morning. He blended in seamlessly.

Jim searched the faces in the buffet line. He sidled up to a young man who openly wore a look of loneliness and desperation in his eyes. For a young businessman, his eyes were strangely void of the greedy glint that is handed out to graduating business school students along with their degrees at convocation.

Jim exchanged small talk with the young businessman as they filled their plates with food. Nobody noticed the dirt and sweat stains on Jim's suit. He piled his plate full with an assortment of grease and potatoes. A tractor engine rumbled in his stomach, threatening to break through the walls. Jim added an extra layer of French fries and gravy on top of his pile, and headed to the nearest table with a few empty seats.

Thinking that Jim was upper management, the desperate young man followed after him like a puppy. Though he was young and innocent, he was still eager to make an ass of himself to get ahead.

Jim dug into his plate of greasy food like an angry hog. He caught himself stuffing a handful of pancakes down his throat and realized he should stop eating like a slob if he wanted to maintain a low profile. Jim picked up his fork and dug it into a stack of bacon. He slowly brought the fork to his mouth. His hand was shaking as he slid the bacon off the fork with his lips.

"Thank you, Jim," his stomach whispered in a quivering voice.

Jim looked up from his food to find that his table was packed full of middle-aged whites, all of whom were currently engaging in middle-aged white conversation: business, politics, laws, rules, money, wife and kids, complaints, cars, coffee, dogs, sports.

They were busy discussing the thrilling topic of yacht sizes when an older lady with grey hair and a gentle face, sitting across from Jim, spoke up. It was at this point that the conversation took a strange turn.

"Many years ago I worked at a paper mill," she began. "And sometimes the kids would come in off the street and ask to use the bathroom. Now, I had no problem with them using our bathroom, but the problem was, our bathrooms were in the basement. So whenever some kids came in, I had to stop what I was doing and take them down to the basement, just to make sure they didn't steal anything or piss all over the floor."

A few whites chuckled awkwardly. Somebody at the other end of the table spoke up. "But what if one of the kids fell down the stairs or something? What if some kid went home and told his parents you tried to molest them? You could get in serious trouble, you know. It'd be your word against theirs in a court of law."

"Well, that's just it," said the lady. All eyes at the table were on her. She looked around from face to face and slowly opened her mouth. "I *am* a child molester."

A stunned silence fell over the table. A moment later everyone burst out into uncontrollable laughter. Jim laughed along with the rest of them while continuing to stuff food into his mouth.

The lady began sobbing uncontrollably, but her sobs were drowned out by the raucous laughter. Nobody noticed her crying. They all continued to laugh and laugh. The lady buried her face in her hands, then when nobody was looking, she picked up her fork and jabbed it into her neck. Blood spurted out all over Jim's French fries.

"Awww," Jim groaned. "That's gross."

Seconds later, Mama Jo came storming out of the kitchen, an ambulance was called, and all the middle-aged whites were kicked out of the restaurant.

Jim found himself back on the street, his stomach only half-full of greasy food.

****

Sheila's hands shook as she pushed the last button through the hole in her collared shirt. She took a deep breath and studied her reflection in the mirror. She pulled down her baseball cap and squared her shoulders. She pushed her shoulders forward and stuck out her gut. Her reflection peered back at her with pity and skepticism. She twitched her fake mustache back and forth and ignored the imploring eyes in the mirror.

Sheila had constructed her mustache by collecting cat hair from the couch cushions and carefully placing the hairs along a strip of double-sided tape.

She looked her reflection up and down and was satisfied with what she saw. She was clad from head to toe in Jim's clothing. She looked like a real bonafide man. Nobody would ever recognize her.

Sheila slipped on Jim's brown leather shoes and tied up the laces. Her disguise kind of made her look like an effeminate Sherlock Holmes. She took a deep breath and exhaled. Her mind was made up. There was no turning back. She was going to get some answers. She was going to get to the bottom of whatever was going on in Turtle Pond. She put her hand on the doorknob and pushed the door open. She stepped boldly forward and the sunlight beamed down, illuminating the tiny particles of dust on her mustache.

****

If you want to retain your belief that people are inherently good and kind, then whatever you do, do not interact with people.

****

Good people are kept busy by bad people. Don't kid yourself- bad people *do* exist. But there aren't as many of them as you'd think.

Bad people run around finding ways to exploit the world, and good people run around trying to fix and reverse the actions of the bad people. The rest of us haven't yet decided if we're good or bad. And so we all keep busy and the world remains in a relatively stable state of equilibrium.

****

As the impossibly compassionate Rilke once said, "Perhaps everything terrible is in its deepest being something helpless that wants help from us."

CHAPTER 18

"Be content with what you have." – *Hebrews 13:5*

****

Karl entered Turtle Pond Butcher Shop to find the butcher, Mr. Meyer, standing behind the counter picking at his teeth with a large gleaming knife. Mr. Meyer saw Karl and put down the knife.

"What can I get for you today, son?"

"Your gums are bleeding," said Karl.

Mr. Meyer grabbed a cloth and wiped the blood from his gums, then threw the cloth into the corner and turned back to Karl.

"I have a question for you," said Karl.

"If you're wondering why I don't have any fresh beef today, it's not my fault," Mr. Meyers raised his hands in defense. "There was a cow riot down in Trenton County, and it's completely out of my hands. It's an absolute mess. Apparently the cows formed some sort of a union, claiming that the farmers refused to recognize their rights as living creatures. And now we have angry, escaped cows running wild all over the country. There's nothing I can do. No fresh beef for miles. But can I offer you some fresh lamb thigh?"

"No thanks," said Karl, looking quizzically at the jittery butcher. "I was actually wondering if you could tell me what a permanium is?"

"Hmm," the butcher furrowed his thick brow, and then furrowed it some more. He licked his still-bleeding gums and swallowed. He slowly unfurled his double-furled brow.

"Well I reckon a permanium is one of those people who feasts on human brains. You know, those nasty buggers who come back to life when you kill them."

Karl wrote this down on his pad as Mr. Meyer eyed him suspiciously.

"For all I know," said Mr. Meyer, leering at Karl, "*you* could be one of them." He walked warily to the counter and picked up a meat cleaver.

Karl thanked Mr. Meyer, and walked inside (outside).

****

Karl's Uncle Kurt passed away on Karl's first day of Grade 3. Uncle Kurt had taught Karl to always enjoy life's happy moments as they were happening.

Karl would often hear his Uncle Kurt quietly saying to himself, "If this isn't nice, I don't know what is."

Karl noticed that Uncle Kurt would utter this phrase at odd times, when nothing significant seemed to be happening, like when the two of them were sitting quietly on the porch, or during a sunset, or while walking slowly down the street, or while watching a bird flit around from one branch to another, or after taking a sip of red wine. It was never anything fantastic that made Uncle Kurt say this phrase.

"If this isn't nice, I don't know what is."

Uncle Kurt once told Karl that if he closed his eyes and let his mind wander, no matter where he was, he would be able to bring himself to a place of peace and contentment.

Karl had taken this advice to heart, and had also taken it a step further. Karl had decided that he would stop looking for things that make him sad or angry. Those things are much too easy to find:

"That person is talking too loud."

"This game is boring."

"It hurts too much."

"It's too noisy."

"I don't like these people."

"I'm not having fun."

Instead, Karl tried to find one small thing that made him happy or grateful or curious or fascinated, in every moment. A smell, a sound, a movement, a beam of light, a shadow, a shape, a texture, a voice, anything that captured his imagination, anything that he could focus his senses on.

No matter where you are, try to find that thing. You can even make a list. You can title it, "Things I like about this moment."

****

Uncle Kurt had passed away at age 56. The doctors couldn't explain why he died. He was in perfect health. It seemed his heart had simply given up one night while he was sleeping.

Aunt Jill, Kurt's wife, revealed at the funeral why she thought Uncle Kurt died. Here is what she said:

"The world finally overwhelmed him." She smiled through her tears. "I'm surprised it took so long."

****

Uncle Kurt had once told Karl a story about a small town where a man named Harry was responsible for firing a cannon every day at exactly 12 o'clock noon. Harry had fired the cannon every day at noon for 22 years.

The people in town didn't even notice the cannon anymore. They didn't hear it when it went *boom*. When the cannon went *boom*, they didn't even flinch. They kept going about what they were doing.

Then one day, when Harry was about to fire the cannon, he had a heart attack and dropped dead. At 12 o'clock noon that day, for the first time in 22 years, the cannon did not go *boom*. The people in town were so surprised by the silence that they nearly jumped out of their skins.

****

A kind word, a silent understanding, a quiet gesture is frightening in a world of angry noise.

****

Arthur sneezed. He wiped the snot from his upper lip with his sleeve. He shook his head and it felt light and empty. He laughed anxiously and mumbled to himself.

"Who am I? I'm not a worm. I'm not an orchid. I'm not a swan."

He went through this checklist one by one. Maybe he could figure out who or what he was by eliminating everything he was not.

"I'm not a cloud. I'm not a pencil. I'm not a piece of gum. I'm me. I'm a person. I'm somebody. I'm nobody... Who am I?"

Arthur continued walking down the street mumbling aloud. He looked up to see an old man pushing a newborn baby in a stroller, heading towards him. The old man wore a grey fedora and black-rimmed glasses. An inverted forest of salt-and-pepper hair emerged from his nostrils.

Everything about the old man was grey and rusted and broken. Everything about the baby was bright and fresh and new. As the old man and the baby drew nearer, Arthur could see that the baby's eyes sparkled with laughter, and he wore a curious smile as if he knew what a ridiculous pair he and the old man made.

Arthur looked at the old man in the grey

fedora pushing the smiling baby in the stroller, and he laughed from deep in his belly, though he did not know why. He made a silly face at the baby. and the baby giggled and hiccupped in response.

Arthur guessed that the baby could help him figure out who he really was, but the baby couldn't talk. Arthur thought to himself, *if only babies could talk, they would fix all the world's problems.*

CHAPTER 19

"Prayer does not change God, but it changes him who prays." – *Soren Kierkegaard*

****

The strange man walked down the street, his eyes darting from side to side. His gait was jerky around the knees, as though he was exerting a great deal of energy to appear to be walking casually. In focusing so intensely on a smooth gait, his movements actually became more stiff and robotic.

The man stroked his mustache and adjusted its positioning on his upper lip with every few steps he took. His plaid shirt bulged out at the chest as if he was wearing a bra. There were bumps and troughs in his clothing in all the wrong places. The only truly manly thing about him was the fact that he had accumulated large pools of sweat under his armpits, which soaked through his shirt to form dark, itchy stains. The strange man walked past an old woman and nodded.

"Good day to you," he said gruffly. He coughed and cleared his throat.

"Oh, why hello there, Sheila" replied the old woman. "I almost didn't recognize you. How are you doing today?"

Sheila didn't respond. She adjusted her mustache back to an even position, tipped her hat to the lady, and walked quickly away.

She could see her destination in the distance: Mayor Cotton's office, which sat on the corner of the main intersection in town. Sheila had planned out what she would do when she arrived at the Mayor's office. She would storm through the big oak doors directly into his office and demand an explanation for why he was trying to exterminate all the permaniums in Turtle Pond.

Just in case Mayor Cotton questioned her about her identity, Sheila had prepared a fake ID badge to prove that she was a powerful man from an important government agency. She had constructed the ID card by writing neatly with a black marker on the back of a piece of cardboard from a cereal box.

"Sheila!" A booming voice rang out like fireworks through the clear crisp air.

Sheila looked across the street to see Ray Goiglecht waving frantically to her. Ray Goiglecht was one of Jim's drinking buddies. A real loud kind of guy who took over every conversation he was a part of. After a few drinks

Ray would often brag about the time he farted so loud he lost four pounds. Ray was known around town for getting obscenely drunk while still maintaining perfect penmanship. His friends and family would often receive letters in the mail that made absolutely no sense, but were very neatly written. For example, here is a drunken letter he wrote to his mother in the midst of a three-day drinking binge:

"Dear Whiskey,
The cat please pooped on the roof again. I told Mary to eat Bermuda but she tap dance with shark. I'm so drink right now. Airplane jumped and laugh!
Kiss me, lazy Susan."

It was written in lovely flowing cursive.

Ray made to cross the street towards Sheila, but was forced to wait as a large transport truck passed by. Sheila took the opportunity to dart into the nearest alley. She ripped off her mustache and stuffed it inside her jacket pocket. She emerged on the other side of the alley onto a small street lined with houses. She took a few steps and bumped headlong into George, the town grocer.

"Hey Sheila!" said George. George looked Sheila up and down and grinned stupidly. "Trying out a new style are we?" said George.

Sheila's lips pursed and her cheeks reddened. She turned and hurried down the street back towards her house. She felt embarrassed and naked, like a thousand pairs of eyes were watching her every move. She loosened her hips and began to walk like a lady again. She removed her hat and let her hair down. She rushed the rest of the way home in her husband's clothing, feeling quite silly.

****

Sheila once wrote a story about multiple universes. Here is the basic premise:

There are trillions upon trillions upon trillions upon trillions of universes just like ours. Within every atom in our universe is an unseeable universe just like ours. And indeed, our universe exists inside a single atom in a larger universe. And that larger universe exists inside a single atom in an even larger universe. And so on, forever.

Most universes are very similar to ours, having only one or two obvious differences. For example, in one universe people speak in colours. In another universe, people sleep when the sun is out and wake up when the moon rises. In another universe, everyone's genitals stick out of their foreheads. In another universe, everyone lives inside volcanoes. In another universe, people have three legs and ten arms, with one finger at the end of each arm. In another universe, all the humans look and act like dogs, and each dog guards a wooden shed full of money. If a dog comes too close to another dog's shed, a fight ensues in which the dogs attempt to sink their razor-sharp teeth into one another's neck. When the dogs growl or bark at each other, drool dribbles down and forms puddles on the ground. Sometimes, flowers spring up in the puddles of drool. The dogs quickly devour the lovely flowers, and shit them back out as stringy brown excrement.

At the time when Sheila wrote this story, humans in our universe didn't know that alternate universes existed. Hell, they didn't even know that their own universe was teeming with all sorts of life forms (this would not be discovered until the invention of the laser-beam space ship in 2159).

In 2159, humans in our universe will be astonished to discover that all other life within their universe speaks one dialect, which is Hebrew. We are the lone species that does not exclusively speak Hebrew. This discovery will spark a global conversion where all people on earth adopt Hebrew as their first language. In November 2061, the President of the United Universal Affairs Committee will, rather redundantly, declare Hebrew the official language of the universe.

One thing that humans in our universe may never find out is that our universe is the only universe that is called a "universe." Every other universe has their own name for the vast unknowable thing that their reality exists within.

****

In one particular universe (I would tell you its name, but it cannot be translated into English), every detail is practically identical to our universe, except that everybody on *their* earth-like planet is born without freedom.

Some people, however, have figured out how to attain freedom. The only catch is that every time a person attains freedom, they suddenly and mysteriously vanish in the middle of the night, and are never heard from again, as though some secret clan of ninjas had come and stolen them away.

The people who are left behind try everything to figure out how to attain freedom. They try working harder, laughing louder, eating different types of food, talking more, talking less, buying lots of shiny stuff, going to church, exercising more, relaxing more, painting pictures, listening to loud music, hugging obsessively, but nothing seems to work, none of these things seem to lead to freedom. Every once in a while a person gets a special tingling feeling while painting a picture or playing the piano, and becomes convinced that they have finally found freedom, and will soon be taken away in the middle of the night. They are always disappointed when they awake in the morning, lying in the same old bed, next to the same old person.

But every once in a while, when people least expect it, another person attains freedom and disappears in the middle of the night.

Some people claim that immediately before a person attains freedom, they become strangely quiet and fail to speak to anyone for a number of days. Because of this, many people regard silent, introverted people with suspicion, and keep a close watch on them.

Virtually nothing is known about how a person attains freedom, or where they go after they do. There are no books written about it, and nothing is spoken of it but pure rumor and speculation. I can't tell you how the people in this universe attain freedom, but I *have* been given permission to tell you where they go when they do.

When a human attains freedom they are whisked off into the night by a group of silent, ninja-like beings (yes, the ninja rumours are true). The human is drugged, blindfolded, tied and gagged. They are thrown into a silent hover-vehicle and hurried off to a secret location, where they are strapped into a large machine and zapped to another universe. Upon arrival in this new universe, the human is lowered by crane into a small, sterile white room occupied by two other humans, who have also recently attained freedom. Inside the room are three desks, one large and two small, three padded chairs, one comfortable and two slightly less comfortable, and a thin, inward-opening flap in the wall, just large enough for a plate of macaroni to be passed through.

The entire universe consists of millions of identical white rooms lined up side-by-side, covering the surface of every planet.

Before being lowered into the white room, the humans' memories are completely erased so that when they reawake, they are like newborn babies, innocent and pure, believing that the desks and chairs, and the two other humans, and the white walls surrounding them are the entirety of their universe.

When one of the humans grows old and dies, they are immediately replaced.

CHAPTER 20

"Everywhere across whatever sorrows of which our life is woven, some radiant joy will gaily flash past." – *Nikolai Gogol*

****

Like a bulimic food critic, Jim's stomach had rejected Mama Jo's greasy cooking, and tossed it up all over the sidewalk just a few steps away from the front door of Mama Jo's.

Now, after nearly three hours of tireless walking, Jim found himself two towns closer to Paxton. He plopped down on a hard curb for a moment's rest. His stomach grumbled angrily in Spanish. Jim dug in his pockets to check if any money had magically appeared since the last time he checked. His hands came out empty.

Jim looked up and saw a group of three fat people- one fat lady and two fat men- walking towards a diner with a neon sign. One of the fat men strayed behind, gasping and puffing loudly. He couldn't keep up with the pace of the other two fat people. Jim studied the trailing fat man. A thick layer of excess fat spilled out over the man's pants, acting like a blubbery belt that held his pants up by pressing them tightly against his waist. One advantage of being grotesquely overweight is that you don't have to buy a belt.

With their slow, swaying gaits, the three oversized humans appeared almost reluctant to enter the diner. Like condemned inmates shuffling down the narrow prison hallway for the last time, they waddled slowly but willingly toward their deaths.

They all wanted the same thing. They were all attempting to fill the food-shaped hole inside them.

We all have a hole inside us. But everyone's hole is a different shape. For some, the hole is shaped like God. For others it's shaped like sex, or drugs, or music, or knowledge, or ignorance.

A particularly delicious hole is one that's shaped like a slice of carrot cake. It's easy to fill, but it empties very quickly.

****

The straggling fat man finally reached the diner and squeezed himself through the doorway. The door slammed ominously shut behind him.

A homeless man appeared from behind Jim and tapped him on the shoulder. "Spare change?" he said.

Jim was startled for a moment, and then responded by using a phrase that had gotten him out of many precarious situations in his life. He looked up at the homeless man and said, "I really do care, but I don't have any money."

This time it was true.

****

I once had a dream in which a Russian man named Ivan said to me, "Life is one big jar of jam, and we are all fermenting inside."

****

The sun kissed the crest of the horizon. With every breath it took, the earth sucked the sun further and further down into its tired lungs. A little bird flitted miles away, ascending to drill a hole through the clouds that washed across the sky like white rapids.

Arthur strolled down the street and came upon an old man tending his garden. "Flowers are looking good, sir!" Arthur called out.

"Shut up," said the old man. He stared at Arthur with steely grey eyes. The old man's face was droopy and sad, and his voice was gruff like a dog's bark.

Arthur continued down the street, whistling and kicking pebbles, with no idea where he was going.

CHAPTER 21

"I didn't know which way to go,
But the wind blew hard toward one side,
And I followed in the way it pushed me."
– *Fernando Pessoa*

****

Karl was on his way to visit Mayor Cotton. If anyone in Turtle Pond really knew what a permanium was, it was Mayor Cotton.

As Karl walked along, strange thoughts and memories swirled around in his head. He thought back to the day when he had been sitting alone with his grandfather in the hospital. It was the day before his grandfather died. His grandfather had opened his eyes and slowly turned his head to Karl.

"This is the story of life," he had said. "You hope to meet a lovely girl, and you hope to avoid an angry man, and there is nothing you can do to guarantee that either will happen. Good luck."

****

The night after his grandfather said those words, Karl went home and began to write a short book that he could read aloud to comfort his old dying grandfather. Karl only managed to write two pages before his grandfather died. Here is what he wrote:

"You are walking down a peaceful path.
You do not know where you are going.
But when you get there, the trees will dance.
The grass will sing in chorus.
The birds will whistle and perch on your shoulders.
Everyone you have ever loved will be there.
They will all be smiling and speaking in poetry.

A glowing lady will come give you a hug.
You will lose yourself in her embrace.
She is the mother of the universe.
She gave birth to you.
She loves you more than all of her other

creations.
Imagine what it will feel like,
When she holds you,
To know that you are loved."

****

Many years later, at the age of 37, Karl would take this book out of the drawer and finish writing it. It would be 21 pages long and titled, "The Book of the Dead." Here is the last paragraph from "The Book of the Dead":

"Death is a dream,
With music and dancing trees.
If you wish to turn it off and just sleep,
You can do that too."

****

Karl's grandfather had died in his sleep. What a nice way to go. Dreaming, dreaming, dreaming.

****

Dreaming.

****

Isn't it funny how we die so peacefully? We die so quietly. After a life of movement and noise, we go out without so much as a peep. We go out with one final breath. The last noise we make could easily be mistaken for a gust of wind.

****

Why do we die so peacefully? Because if every living thing let out a scream when its heart stopped beating, we would all go deaf.

****

Karl rode his thoughts like a magic carpet all the way to Mayor Cotton's office. He strolled past the receptionist and tapped his knuckles on Mayor Cotton's door.

"Come in," came a velvety smooth voice from within.

Karl swung the door open and stepped inside the expansive office. He noticed the smell right away. Mayor Cotton's office smelled like stale garlic bread and lemon juice. He also noticed the toy train that clattered noisily around the room on a loop of metal tracks.

The toy train let out a humble toot and emitted a tiny puff of steam from its miniature whistle. Mayor Cotton did not look up at Karl. He was focused intensely on the train. "Yes, yes... yes," he whispered loudly. "Yes... Perfect... It's perfect."

Karl cleared his throat and Mayor Cotton jerked his head upward. His eyes lost their insane gleam, and he immediately clothed his face with a perfectly tailored politician's smile.

"Hello there, son," he said. "What can I do for you today?" Mayor Cotton flattened out his hair with the palm of his hand, and waited for Karl to respond.

"Well sir," said Karl. "I'll get straight to the point. I'd like to know what a permanium is. I'd like to know what's so great about permaniums.

I'd like to know why we're celebrating them for an entire week. If you'll just give me a simple explanation, I'll be on my way, and you can get back to your... erm... train."

Mayor Cotton paused for a moment, staring thoughtfully at the train. He loved that train more than his own mother.

"Let me tell you a story," he said, and took a deep breath. "Imagine your finger is bitten off by a snapping turtle."

Karl nodded his head.

"Now, imagine the snapping turtle regurgitates your finger into the ocean where it is eaten by a large trout. Then, before the trout has time to digest your finger, a storm comes along and the trout is washed up onto shore."

"Okay," Karl nodded.

"The very next day, a starving child finds the trout laying on the sand and cooks it for dinner. The trout, with your finger inside, saves the child from starving to death. Now, does the knowledge that your finger provided sustenance for a starving child make the pain of losing your finger any less painful?"

"Uh... You lost me there," said Karl.

"What I'm asking is," said Mayor Cotton, "does pain still feel like pain if you're helping another person in the process? Can an otherwise painful act feel painless with the knowledge that you are helping another human being?" He paused and looked at Karl, as if realizing for the first time who he was speaking to. "Perhaps you're too young to understand," he trailed off.

Karl pondered this for a moment. "Well, I'm not sure if you can think away pain," he said.

"Maybe you can with practice. But if for every painful experience that occurred to a person, an equally joyful experience was to occur to someone else, then I guess the universe would be a much more balanced place than it is. I guess pain would be a little bit easier to bear."

"Aha!" said Mayor Cotton. "But how do you know that that's not true? What if the universe holds a perfect balance between joy and sorrow, between positive and negative, between poverty and affluence, between suffering and pain, but we humans are too busy focusing on the sorrow to notice the joy all around us?"

"But what does this have to do with permaniums?" asked Karl.

"Don't you see?" said Mayor Cotton. "Permaniums have to constantly prick themselves with painful needles in order to make sure their blood levels are okay. Because of their pain, the universe is obligated to create and manifest an equal and proportional amount of pleasure somewhere else in the world.

"We should be thankful for permaniums, because for every time one of them stabs a syringe into their finger, or into their buttocks, a little boy's father buys him a new puppy."

Karl was utterly confused.

Mayor Cotton smiled knowingly at Karl. "You're a smart kid, but you've got a lot to learn." He turned to look at his train as he continued speaking to Karl. "To answer your original question, we are celebrating permaniums because permaniums supply the world with joy."

****

To each his own eccentricities.

****

It was dark inside (outside). Jim stretched out on the hard park bench and wrapped the darkness around him like a blanket. The blanket was thick and soft, obviously knit by an 86-year-old Polish woman.

Jim saw a pillow floating lazily through the air just a few inches from his face. The pillow was being gently pushed along by an inky wind. Jim reached out and snatched the pillow, staining his hand with ink in the process. He stuffed the pillow under his head before it had a chance to float away. He felt comfortable now with his dark blanket and his lazy pillow.

Jim gazed up at the moon. The moon looked down at him. Jim felt that he and the moon had a shared understanding. About what, he did not know. All he knew was that he had never felt so close to the moon in his life.

The moon flickered and turned off and Jim realized that he had been staring at a lamppost and not at the moon. Jim shook his head and laughed.

"If it's so easy to mistake the moon for a lamppost, then maybe the moon isn't so special," said Jim. "Or maybe lampposts deserve more credit than they get."

Jim searched the sky until he found the real moon. He verified that it was the real moon by checking to make sure that it did not have a pole attached to it.

"So," Jim addressed the moon. "Are you

stupid? Or are lampposts smart?"

When the moon did not answer, Jim laid back his head and drifted off to sleep. He was immediately thrown into the middle of an intensely vivid dream. In his dream, Jim mistook a shoe for a dog. He mistook a street for a river. He mistook a kite for a strange bird. He mistook a baseball for an apple. He mistook a piano for a dinosaur. He mistook a piece of string for a rainbow.

Jim abruptly awoke and saw that the moon had been watching him sleep. Jim propped himself up on one elbow. "Am I really stupid?" he asked the moon. "Or is the world stupid?"

"No," said the moon. "You're stupid."

CHAPTER 22

"Only believers have any reason to fear death, my child; always between heaven and hell, not knowing which will open to receive them, they're torn by anxiety. As for me, I hope for nothing, and I'm sure of being no more unhappy after my death than I was before my life." – *Marquis de Sade*

****

140

A Short History of Unnecessary Death and Strawberries Produced

Location	Year	Dead	Strawberries (1,000 Metric tons)
Europe	1915	50,000,000	568.94
Europe	1946	70,000,000	794.95
Korea	1953	3,000,000	88.44
Vietnam	1975	5,000,000	1.67
Ethiopia	2000	123,000	0.42
Eritria	2000	19,000	0.12
Congo	2003	5,000,000	0.21
Iraq	2006	100,000	27.0
Sudan	2008	400,000	0.00
Afghanistan	2009	2,000,000	3.10

****

Ho hum. Please pass the chocolate covered strawberries.

****

The worst thing for monkeys would be if we started treating them like humans.

****

Arthur stumbled toward the light. He came closer and closer until he could read the words on the neon sign. They read: "Peterville All-Night Diner."

Arthur walked through (in) the front doors

of the dingy diner and looked around. Vagrants, bums and drunks were scattered around the diner like sleepy fireflies, sprawled across booths and benches, and perching heavily atop yellow padded stools. Arthur chose a booth close to the door and flopped down in a daze. He was completely lost and confused.

"What can I get for you honey?" asked the waitress, looking down at Arthur with tired eyes.

Arthur looked up at her and smiled a wide, goofy smile. He thought for sure he had found his mother.

"Shouldn't you be at home in bed?" asked the waitress.

Arthur smiled wider.

"Are you lost?"

Arthur leaned back and sneezed five times. Five violent sneezes.

"God bless you," said the waitress. She handed Arthur a tissue.

The bearded man in the booth behind Arthur suddenly jerked awake from his slumber. He shot out of his seat and gave the waitress a big hug. The waitress pulled away politely and stood staring warily at the man.

"You know," said the bearded man, "one of the nicest things a person can say is God Bless You." The bearded man's eyes were wild like an airplane pilot trying to pull up out of a nosedive. He reeked of whiskey. "To say God Bless You is to truly wish someone the best, to wish them happiness, to wish that they would be treated with kindness. I'm not only talking about saying God Bless You when someone sneezes, or when saying goodbye, or when signing a greeting card. Much of that is thoughtless and just for show." The bearded man was speaking rapidly now, struggling to purge his head of these thoughts so he could go back to sleep.

"When we see the whole world dying and feel helpless, it's nice to know that we can still have good intentions, that we can still wish others well, that we can still want for others to be happy, that we can still say God Bless You and really mean it.

"All of our frustrations amount to nothing but hot air, but our frustrations are honest. We *should* be frustrated. We *should* be embarrassed to be human. We *should* wish the world was a little bit more perfect." The bearded man took off his hat and held it against his chest. He turned his piercing eyes to Arthur and stared at him with an intense angry love.

"Can I tell you a secret?" The bearded man was nearly whispering now, his voice hoarse with whiskey and wool. He leaned in close to Arthur. The waitress leaned in to hear the man's words.

"The world *is* perfect in music," the bearded man whispered. "It is only when the music stops that the world falls apart."

Arthur sneezed again, five times.

"God bless you," said the man. He slumped back down in his booth and fell asleep.

Arthur and the waitress stared silently at the man who had just become animated before their eyes. His chest rose and fell slowly like a wolf lying safe and warm in his den. He snored in loud horse-breaths.

Suddenly, there was a loud bang on the table. Arthur looked up to see the caped man from the church standing in front of him with his giant palms lying flat on the table. Instead of wearing the scarlet cape from before, the man now wore a full three-piece suit and held a corncob pipe between his teeth.

"Dad?" said Arthur.

The caped man ignored Arthur and began yelling at the top of his lungs, waving his corncob pipe in the air. "I overheard that utterly idiotic conversation you just had, and I must say that I could not disagree more with everything that was said. To say God Bless You is not an act of kindness. No, to say God Bless You implies that God has not already blessed you, that you are in need of his blessings, that God has not blessed you as much as he has blessed me, that God would not bless you unless I asked him to, as a personal favor from him to me. I must be in a higher position than you, socially, economically or in my own opinion, to bestow God's blessings upon you.

"And it makes me feel so good to do so. Oh, I feel like such a kind person when I say God Bless You to a poor runny-nosed soul in the street. It makes me feel all tingly inside to convince myself that I can sway God's blessings, that I can convince him to bless who I see fit, that I can borrow his magical powers every time someone sneezes.

"To utter these three simple words, God Bless You, simultaneously eases my guilt, quiets my conscience, caresses my fragile ego and shelters me from my own ignorance. Yes, God's blessings move in only one direction, from the blessed to the unblessed, from the rich to the poor, from the privileged to the depraved, from those who are close to God to those who are not."

Arthur sneezed three times.

The caped man stared down at him with disdain. "I sincerely hope you never sneeze again," he said. He stuck the corncob pipe back between his teeth. He blew out a few soapy bubbles and rushed inside (outside).

CHAPTER 23

"Those stinkers in Country No. 2! We're going to board them and cut their livers out! Let's go! Let's go! We've got everything we need on board! All together now! Let's hear you shout so the deck trembles: 'Long live Country No. 1!' So you'll be heard for miles around. The man that shouts the loudest will get a medal and a lollipop!"
– *Louis-Ferdinand Celine*

****

Jim pried his eyes open with his fingers. His eyelids were heavy and full of fluid. Jim rubbed his face and watched as bits of dirt fell from his beard like ground pepper onto his chest.

He picked himself up and dragged himself into a nearby coffee shop. He ordered a glass of water in hopes that it would satisfy his rumbling stomach. The waitress took one look at Jim's tired, dirty face, and poured him a full mug of steaming black coffee.

"It's on the house," she said and pushed the coffee across the counter. Tears welled up in Jim's eyes.

"What an angel you are," he said to the waitress. He wanted to leap over the counter and hug her, to squeeze her angelic shoulder blades together with all his might.

The waitress was called over to a table and Jim took a seat by the front window. He stared at the empty street outside and felt a strange painless pain inside his chest. He realized that he missed his family.

They must be worried sick about me, thought Jim. He felt a twinge of guilt for having left so suddenly, without telling them where he was going, or for how long he would be gone.

Jim closed his eyes and imagined little Karl and Arthur huddled together in the living room hugging each other and crying out between sobs, "Daddy! Daddy! Where's Daddy? Where did Daddy go?"

Sweet little Karl. Sweet little Arthur.

A hot tear leaked down Jim's cheek and disappeared into his beard.

Jim imagined Sheila standing beside Karl and Arthur, attempting to be strong, trying to console her children. "It's okay children. Daddy still loves you. Daddy's in a better place now." She was crying too.

Oh, Dear sweet Sheila.

Jim imagined dozens of policemen running around the house, flipping over couch cushions, rummaging through drawers, and stretching their necks to look behind the TV for clues, searching for any sign of where Jim had gone. Occasionally an officer would yell out "I think I found a clue!" or "Here's something!" Then one officer would say to Sheila, "Ma'am, did your husband have any enemies that you are aware of?" or, "Did he have any secrets?" or, "Did your husband have any ties to the Mob?"

Sheila cried and cried.

Jim sighed and smiled a sad, courageous smile. He knew that when he returned home with his stockpile of shampoo, his family would understand that he *had* to go on this journey. He had no choice. He knew they would be relieved and grateful that he was alive, and would take him back with open arms.

Jim only hoped his family would have the strength to carry on without him until then.

****

Sheila heard a noise in the kitchen and tiptoed cautiously down the stairs. She peeked around the corner to see Karl rummaging through the fridge.

"Oh, hey Karl," said Sheila.

"Hey mom," said Karl.

"Shouldn't you be at school?"

"No, they gave us the week off."

"Oh."

Karl pulled out a piece of chicken and a chunk of cheddar cheese and thunked them down onto the countertop.

"Where's Arthur?" asked Sheila.

"He's probably at school," said Karl.

"Oh," said Sheila.

Neither of them had noticed that Jim had

been missing for more than two days.

****

One of Sheila's old short stories was about a man and a woman in a coffee shop. The woman was pregnant. The man was very tall. They had never met before.

The pregnant woman sat alone at a small table drinking a cup of tea.

The man bought a coffee and as he walked past the pregnant woman, he tripped over her bag and spilled scalding hot coffee all over her bulging stomach.

The woman screamed and jumped around while the man did his best to dry off her stomach with his sleeve.

"Dry me off! Dry me off!" The woman screamed hysterically.

The man swiped at her stomach like a maniac.

"Take me to the hospital, quick!" the woman screamed. "I don't want my baby to get FCS!" She was not as worried about the severe burns on her skin as she was about her baby getting FCS, whatever that was.

So they got into the man's car and rushed off to the hospital. When the pregnant woman had calmed down a bit, the man asked her what FCS was.

"Fetal Caffeine Syndrome," she replied briskly.

The man laughed loudly. "That's ridiculous," he said. He was relieved that the woman's baby could not possibly catch this imaginary disease.

"Yeah, well what do you know?" scoffed the pregnant woman with the burnt stomach.

"Even if FCS were real," said the man, "I doubt you could get it by me spilling coffee on your stomach."

"Just shut up and drive."

When they arrived at the hospital an ER doctor took one look at the woman's stomach and said, "Ooh, those are some nasty burns. What happened?"

"He spilled coffee on me," the woman pointed accusingly at the balding man.

"Oh dear," said the doctor, shaking his head. "Looks like a possible case of FCS."

CHAPTER 24

"I have no money, no resources, no hopes. I am the happiest man alive." - *Henry Miller*

****

A single solitary cloud hung in the sky. It was not a pretty cloud. It was torn and raggedy, barely held together, like a dishcloth after years of use. Everybody that saw the lonely cloud felt sorry for it, but there was nothing anybody could do to help it. The cloud would have to suffer all alone, on the stage of the sky, in the spotlight of the sun.

Karl walked past Turtle Pond Library and

peered in through the front window. He saw rows and rows of books, but not a single person, except for old Mrs. Beard who had been the librarian there since before books were invented.

If people were really thoughtful, our libraries would be like zoos. They would have to kick people out due to overcapacity.

Karl considered dropping in to speak with Mrs. Beard, but decided to continue walking. He had other people he wanted to speak with first.

Karl looked up to see his mother's best friend, Jacqueline Snadjman, walking briskly down the sidewalk towards him.

Jacqueline noticed Karl and her face lit up. "Karl, darling! How are you?" said Jacqueline, pinching Karl's cheeks with her clammy fingers.

"Good," said Karl. He was shocked that this lady had actually remembered who he was.

"How is your mother doing? I haven't seen her around lately. Is she alright?"

"I'm not sure," said Karl. "She's been acting kind of strange since permanium awareness week began."

"Do you think she might be sick?" asked Jacqueline.

"Well," said Karl, "when I asked her if she knew what a permanium was, she looked like she was about to throw up. Maybe she dislikes permaniums, or maybe she's uncomfortable talking about them..."

"Oh, dear," said Jacqueline. She was dismayed to hear this news that her best friend Sheila, normally so reserved and tolerant, was seemingly repulsed by permaniums.

"That just won't do," she shook her head and stood silently for a moment with a worried look on her face. "I think I'll pay your mother a visit tonight after dinner," she said. "There are some things I need to teach her about permaniums. And I have something I need to return to her anyways."

Jacqueline Snadjman said goodbye and walked off briskly in the direction of Karl's house.

The lonely cloud set aside the deck of cards and began to assemble a jigsaw puzzle.

****

Arthur had been happily dreaming about a talking cow conducting a train full of cowboys. The cow blew the steam whistle to warn his mother to get off the tracks. His mother looked up and smiled at her son, the conductor. She was so proud of him. Meanwhile, the cowboys played poker in the passenger cars and complimented each other's cowboy boots.

Arthur was awoken from this dream by two loud voices arguing with each other only inches from his ear. He peered out through sticky slitted eyelids to see a man and a woman, both in their mid-thirties, both tall and thin, sitting across from each other at the edge of the booth. Arthur remained in the position he had fallen asleep in, sitting against the wall in the booth with his head resting on the table. He was penned in by the two quarrelers, and would have had to interrupt their quarrel if he wanted to escape.

The man and woman were arguing loudly,

and the other coffee-addicted morning patrons were looking on unenthusiastically. Arthur sneezed, but the couple didn't notice. Their argument was coming to a climax.

"Just tell me the truth, Jason. Do you love me or not?" said the girl, blinking through rapidly forming tears.

"The truth is offensive, Kara," Jason replied calmly.

"What's that supposed to mean?" asked Kara.

"Well Kara," said Jason. "It's like this. I love you, but I can't love you if I have to see you every day. If I have to see you every day, I'm likely to get sick of you in no time."

"You're a real jerk, Jason," said Kara.

"You see!" Jason threw his hands up in despair. "I shouldn't have told you the truth. I should've just lied to you and told you that I love you. You see what I mean? We suppress the truth because it's offensive." Jason then took Kara's hand and raised it to his lips. "I love you Kara," he said.

Kara's lips quivered and she burst into tears. She slid out of the booth and rushed inside (outside).

Arthur saw his chance and escaped from the booth.

****

The doorbell sang out like a retarded bird. Sheila came creeping slowly down the stairs. Her face was stained with dry black riverbeds of makeup. When she reached the bottom of the stairs, she lowered herself down on her hands and knees and began to crawl like a jungle cat towards the front window. She reached up and pulled the blinds apart with a single, shaky finger. Through the crack in the curtains, Sheila could see a figure standing in front of her door. Sheila gasped, and the figure's head jerked towards the window. Sheila quickly ducked and hid behind the wall. Her breathing was fast and heavy. She could not believe what she was seeing. Was this a mirage? Was this really happening?

Outside on the front porch stood Sheila's best friend, Jacqueline Snadjman, waiting patiently, holding a large shiny knife behind her back.

Sheila took a deep breath and counted to ten. She peeked back out the window. Once again Jacqueline jerked her head towards the window. Sheila dove to the floor and laid flat on her stomach. Her entire body was shaking. She was sure that Jacqueline had seen her.

The doorbell rang again, followed by three rapid knocks on the door. Sheila jumped to her feet and dashed up the stairs as fast as her legs would carry her. She threw a brown leather suitcase onto the bed and began tossing things into it. A pair of pants, a few shirts, a handful of underwear. The dry riverbeds on her cheeks filled up again.

****

Out on the front porch, Jacqueline Snadjman turned around and headed down the walkway. She thought she had seen Sheila peering out the front window, but it may have only been something moving in the reflection.

Jacqueline looked down at the cake cutter in her hand and shrugged. She would have to speak with Sheila about permaniums some other time. In the meantime, she would hold onto Sheila's cake cutter for her.

****

Sheila once wrote a story about a man who decided to stop making sense. The moral of the story, if the story had a moral (and all stories must), was: If your way works just as well as the old way, and if your way makes just as much sense as the old way, then why not do it your way?

The man was always miserable at birthday parties, and often broke out into tears at the sound of the "Happy Birthday" song.

He was overjoyed at funerals, wearing his brightest, most colorful suit and saying things like, "Nice weather today," and, "I just bought this shirt last week." He was the only person to ever dance at funerals. No matter how hard he tried to convince others to join him, no one ever did.

When someone took a photograph of the man, he would do his best to re-enact an arbitrary daily activity such as sitting on the toilet or raking leaves on the lawn. He would look up at the camera with a surprised expression, as though the photographer had caught him in a candid moment while emptying his bowels or raking up leaves.

Whenever anyone asked his opinion on anything, the man would respond with the opposite answer the person was expecting (or fishing for). If a friend asked his opinion on a new jacket or pair of pants, he would immediately cringe and say, "I've seen better sights come out of a grizzly bear's ass."

The man would often wear his clothes inside-out, but only on days when it suited his fancy. If he decided to wear his pants rightside-in, he would pull out the pockets so that two long pieces of fabric hung down from his waist like dog ears.

He said goodnight in the morning and good evening at Christmas.

He never wore any socks.

People became outraged at the man's actions and his general disregard for everything that they held as proper, or essential, or part of objective reality, or "the way things are."

Strangers would often say to him, "Why can't you just act normal like everyone else?" The man would respond by throwing an apple up in the air and letting it fall on his head.

****

The story eventually ended when the man was imprisoned for throwing an icecream cone at a purple car.

CHAPTER 25

"Men are jerks. Women are psychotic." – *Kurt Vonnegut*

"Love is the infinite placed within the reach of poodles." – *Louis- Ferdinand Celine*

"I am highly suspicious of love. If somebody says, 'I love you,' to me, I feel as though I had a pistol pointed at my head. What can anybody reply under such conditions but that which the pistol-holder requires? 'I love you, *too*.' The hell with love, and hooray for something else, which I can't even begin to name or describe." - *Kurt Vonnegut*

****

What had Jim been doing for the last two days? Walking. He had been walking for so long that he had forgotten he was walking. He was delirious with hunger and fatigue. His beard was full of foreign specks and splotches. He would drift off into a dream-like state as he trudged along mindlessly, completely losing track of time.

Jim peered down past his beard at his moving feet. He smiled madly at his bare filthy toes, which poked out through the torn fronts of his shoes. He chuckled as his toes slowly transformed into yellow baby ducklings.

The tall grass rustled in the wind, sounding like rolling waves. The sky blurred and merged with the backs of Jim's eyelids. The sound of his footsteps softened and lowered in pitch, turning into the methodical chugging of a passing tugboat.

Jim borrowed binoculars from the stranger next to him, and scanned the deck of the tugboat. An elegant young woman stood at the railing and waved to Jim. She held a newborn child in her arms. Jim smiled and waved back. As Jim peered through the binoculars, the woman calmly tossed the baby over the railing, sending it down, down, down into the thrashing sea. She then resumed waving at Jim as though nothing had happened.

Jim laughed and a string of saliva trickled down into his tangled beard. His feet kept moving. He looked at the road in front of him and saw nothing but endless ocean.

****

Karl collapsed on the grass in tired frustration. He had been wandering around town talking to people all day, and was no closer to discovering what a permanium was. He simply could not find two people who gave him the same answer.

"Permaniums?" said old Mrs. Miller who worked at the drug store. "Aren't those the people who built the pyramids?"

"Oh yeah," said Bill Jamison, who stocked shelves at the grocery store, "those are the guys who patch up your boat if it's got a leak in it."

"I think I saw a permanium running through my yard the other day," said Larry the crossing guard. "Tiny little guys they are, with big beautiful wings. Real fast too."

"Of course, child," said Mrs. Beard the

librarian. "Permaniums are wonderful creatures, who have the ability to camouflage themselves. I believe they're part of the lizard family." Mrs. Beard, of course, was confusing a permanium with a chameleon.

Karl had been keeping a list in his notebook of everything the townspeople told him about permaniums. Here is what it read:

Permaniums:
- are bad people
- should be killed as baby babies
- are different from other people
- can talk to God
- live on trains
- supply the world with joy
- can camouflage themselves
- built the pyramids
- will fix your boat
- have no parents
- only eat carrots
- are zombies
- are fire eaters
- can see the future
- can communicate with animals

****

Arthur could feel miniature woodchucks gnawing away at the supporting beams in his head. His skull felt like it was slowly caving in. To say that Arthur felt *lost* does not accurately describe what he was going through.

Here is a better description: Imagine that one night everybody in the world dreams the same dream. Everybody, that is, except for you.

You don't dream anything. In the dream, everybody learns that pickles are no longer called pickles, but are now called "xanthropes."

The next day, you ask someone to "pass the pickles," and everybody laughs at you. You feel extremely foolish but you don't know why. This scenario is the closest I can come to describing what Arthur had been experiencing ever since he banged his head on Patti LaVernon's table.

****

Arthur stretched his arms toward the café ceiling and groaned. He glided slowly through the rows of booths towards the door.

A conversation at a nearby table caught his ear. He paused next to the table. Two young girls sat across from each other, speaking rapidly and excitedly, and somehow failing to ever make eye contact with one another. Arthur soon caught on to the general pattern of the conversation. The first girl did most of the talking, chattering on like an idiotic squirrel, while the second girl filled in the short gaps by repeating the phrase, "That is *so* funny," over and over again.

Arthur had the feeling that if the first girl got up and walked away, the second girl would continue repeating, "That is *so* funny," at 20-second intervals until the cops came and took her to the nearest mental institution. And if the second girl got up and walked away, the first girl would continue talking to infinity, or at least until there was a sale on at the nearest mall.

****

Most conversation consists of people seeking to affirm their egos, grasping for significance through insincere mutual agreements.

****

Arthur continued toward the door but was once again distracted, this time by two older women who were talking softly in a nearby booth. Arthur slowed his pace and listened while pretending to study the menu above the counter.

One of the ladies was chubby and appeared to be on the verge of tears. The other lady had a full head of bright white hair, and was gently touching the first lady's arm.

"I was devastated when Paul passed away," the chubby lady was saying.

"Well," the older lady responded, "at least you still have that sweet dog of yours to keep you company." The older lady rubbed the chubby lady's arm, which rested heavily on the table. She seemed to very much enjoy rubbing the chubby lady's arm.

"Benji died last week," the chubby lady moaned. "I found him under the back porch. He died all alone... And now I'm going to die alone too. Just like Benji."

"Aww," said the older lady. "It's going to be okay, Glenda." The older lady rubbed the chubby arm back and forth, back and forth. She stared lovingly at the arm.

All this time, Arthur had been inching his

way closer to the table. He cleared his throat and spoke up.

"Someone's always dying," he said. The ladies paused and looked at the young boy who had so rudely interrupted their moment of tenderness and grief.

"Excuse me?" said the older lady, staring at Arthur as though he had a porcupine sitting on his head, or a tuna fish glued to his chin.

"Someone's always dying," Arthur said again. "In fact, three people die every second."

The ladies sat in stunned silence. The older lady's hand was frozen in mid arm-rub.

"Did you know that there are over 10 quintillion insects in the world?" Arthur continued. "That's a 10 with 16 zeroes after it. Can you imagine how many insects die every second? Some locust swarms have over 1 billion locusts. In one swarm!" The words were tumbling forth out of Arthur's mouth.

"And East African termite queens lay an egg every two seconds. That's 43,000 children a day. Can you imagine the massive amounts of death that insects experience on a daily basis? Their brothers and sisters and sons and daughters and parents and cousins are dying by the thousands every single day. But you never see an insect crying about death. You never see a mother spider crying when a son or daughter gets flushed down the toilet. You never see a family of flies holding a ceremony around an old fly-swatter dotted with the corpses of dead family members." Arthur paused for a moment.

"Or maybe insects do mourn death, but their tears are invisible. Or maybe insects have learned that being sad about death is useless, and that if they stopped and mourned every time a friend or family member died, they would never get anything done. Or maybe there is a select group of insects whose job it is to live under ground and mourn the deaths of other insects, and that's why we never see insects crying."

****

Arthur failed to realize that he had just recited facts about insects that he had learned in grade two, facts that he had memorized over three-and-a-half years ago.

****

We all should live with an imaginary dog on our laps.

****

After leaving the restaurant, Arthur was overtaken by an intense fit of dizziness and was forced to sit down on the curb. His body felt weak and he was desperate to find a comfortable place to lay down and rest for a few minutes.

He noticed a nearby tractor-trailer with its rear gate open. Bunches of golden hay stuck out over the rear fender of the truck. Arthur pulled himself up into the back compartment and dragged himself over to a mound of hay. The earthy smells overwhelmed him and immediately lifted his spirits. Arthur curled up as his body sank deeper down into the soft hay. He looked like a baby in a cradle, or a boy in a haystack. Seconds later he was sound asleep and snoring like a cow.

CHAPTER 26

"Boredom: the desire for desires." – *Leo Tolstoy*

****

Thousands of miles away, the sun beat down on the bleached island beaches, as tourists forked over wads of money to have their photograph taken with a parrot on their head.

In a hotel overlooking the ocean, Reynold Reynoldson stepped out of the shower, wrapped himself in a white flannel towel, and picked up the telephone on the fourth ring.

"There's a letter for you at the front desk, Mr. Reynoldson," said the voice on the other end.

"Who's it from?" asked Reynold Reynoldson. He was annoyed at being interrupted during his afternoon shower.

"It's from a Mayor Cotton," said the voice on the telephone. "It looks like some sort of invitation."

"Throw it out," said Reynold, and he hung up the telephone. He snatched a piece of pizza from the open box on the table, and stepped back into the steaming shower.

****

Karl lay back on the grass and studied the list in his notepad. He was especially puzzled by what old Joan Bardchuck had said about permaniums. He couldn't help wondering what happened to all of the baby babies who were killed before they were born. Where did they go?

Maybe, thought Karl, they were transported up to the sky where each of them became a star. Then, maybe, once they became stars, they were given one simple task, and that task was to glow as brightly as they could. And by glowing, the baby babies made people stop for a moment to think about life, and to think about death, and to think about how small they are, and to think about how we're only human, and to think about how we don't really know why we're here or what we're doing, and to think about how wonderful the world is, and to think about how freeing it is to simply not know.

****

It is exhilarating to understand things, but it is more exhilarating to understand nothing.

****

Here is a seemingly irrelevant sidenote that demanded to be written: Karl would finish writing his first book at age 17. It would be titled, "The Evolution of Scissors."

Here is an excerpt from the first chapter of

that book:

"I prefer to hide, to be alone and invisible. In a group you are expected to smile. You are expected to fit in. You are expected to act in a way pre-determined by your appearance. You are expected to be happy and stupid if you are young. If you are old, you are expected to walk slow and poop your pants. In a group you must smile because if you don't, they will sense it- they will sense that you are a dysfunctional member of the clan. They will sense it using some sort of sick, collective radar designed to seek out and judge anything reeking of indifference and freedom. Smile. You must smile. Why should you be free while they are trapped behind their masks?"

****

There is a difference between a forced smile and a fake smile. A forced smile is self-sacrificing while a fake smile is pure evil.

****

Karl had always been confused as to why he wasn't interested in doing any of the jobs he saw the adults around him doing. He hadn't yet discovered that nobody really wants to be a lawyer or a plumber or a dentist. People simply become these things because they'd rather be a doctor or a dentist than be a car salesman or an accountant, or vice versa.

Over a number of years, the dull knife of time works its way through the tender meat of our minds, until we come to believe that it is our destiny, our life's purpose, to clean people's teeth or to serve them greasy food, or to clean up people's garbage.

Deep down, nobody really wants to be anything. We are all *forced* to choose. We must all choose to do what sounds the *least least* appealing- that is, assuming you have a choice at all.

As Charles Bukowski once wrote, "The problem is you have to keep choosing between one evil and another."

****

What's really wild is that we *made* these jobs. We created this system of greed. We did it to ourselves. It's absolutely mind-boggling. We put ourselves into these cages. We stole our own freedom. Why have we done this?

That we torture ourselves, put ourselves into this form of economic, spirit-killing slavery should paint an accurate picture of how dumb we really are as a species.

We willingly subject ourselves to boxes of glass and steel that we build with our own hands. We look out and see the birds gliding through the air, the dogs humping joyfully on the street, the monkeys climbing and leaping from tree to tree, and we laugh and say, "What do they know about making money?"

We get a corner office, or an office with a window, an office with a nice view of the grey landscape teeming with drug-addicted mice, and we congratulate ourselves, we think we've done well, we think we've accomplished something.

****

We were all tricked at birth.

****

In the darkness that enshrouded Turtle Pond, a lone figure stood at the side of the main road. A small suitcase rested on the ground nearby. The long-haired creature held out a shaky arm and stuck a thumb up into the air.

After a few minutes, a transport truck emerged from the fog and rumbled to a stop. The door opened, the stranger climbed in, and the truck disappeared down the road.

****

If rats had huge, adorable saucer-plate eyes instead of small, black, beady eyes, we wouldn't kill thousands of them in science labs every year.

CHAPTER 27

"This person sits in a corner and doesn't participate in the conversation but still makes his presence felt and, despite his silence, plays a distinct role in the group. It's because he is dressed in a certain way, because he is so uncommunicative, because he looks at the others with such an empty and indifferent expression, and because he is a nobody, that he contributes to the gathering just by his presence." – *Knut Hamsun*

****

"Ain't it a shame, we learn and learn and die. Ain't it a shame, we learn and learn and learn and die. Ain't it a shame, we learn and learn and die."

This is what Jim was muttering as he stumbled down the center of the road. Cars sped by on both sides, blaring their horns and coming dangerously close to smashing him to pieces.

Nearly three days had passed since Jim had eaten a proper meal. He was no longer seeing straight. He had passed the point of physical longing, the point where the body becomes numb to its unconscious demands.

The highest point of joy rests on the precipice of death on a windy day. This is the point when painful depravity turns into delirious pleasure, when our bodies realize that there is more to be had in denying our senses than in giving in to our needs.

You think celibate priests lead difficult lives? You are mistaken. They are the happiest people on earth! They fool us by putting on sad airs, but in reality they are hoarders of pleasure, they wish to disguise the whirlwind of young lust that is hidden just behind their pupils. Their glass is not empty, because they do not even have a glass.

Jim felt like a priest, a holy man. He lifted his hands and blessed the vehicles as they whizzed by. Drivers yelled out obscenities, and Jim heard, "Hallelujah," and, "Glory to God on the highest."

Jim felt a deep longing in his chest again. He knew that he was going to heaven soon, and that when he arrived, Saint Peter and John the Baptist and maybe even Jonah would be there to greet him and give him a giant, glowing bottle of shampoo. Jim would smile and shake hands with Peter, John and Jonah one by one.

Jim was not aware that the Supreme Court of Angels had voted 5 to 4 in favor of sending Jonah to hell.

Jim raised his eyes and saw his heavenly chariot awaiting him. Strapped to the front were four majestic, white stallions. They were neighing and stamping their feet, anxious to carry Jim up into the clouds.

Jim approached the chariot amid screeching tires and sounds of metal crashing against metal. Jim nodded to one of the stallions and it winked back at him. Jim climbed into the passenger seat and smiled at the white-tuxedo-wearing driver.

"Take me to heaven, Jeeves," said Jim.

****

Multiple witnesses watched as Jim climbed into a white convertible car that was stopped at a red light. They saw Jim push the driver out onto the street, slam the door, and peel out, yelling, "Hyah! Hyah!"

****

Here is a bit of trivial information in what is surely the most insignificant section of this story:

Mr. Matthews had once told Karl's class that the first ever extreme sport was invented by an African cannibal vegetarian tribe called the Pa'Quahs. They only ate humans and vegetables, and also human vegetables.

The Pa'Quahs would tame small dinosaurs to keep as pets, and large dinosaurs to use for transportation. The large dinosaurs would leave monstrous mounds of pooh all over the place.

Mr. Matthews told his class that dinosaur pooh used to be a huge problem. Mounds of pooh would block the main roads, and would seep into the water supply and stink up the entire community.

Mr. Matthews also mentioned to his class that some enterprising Neanderthal could have made a killing by inventing dinosaur-sized litter boxes.

The Pa'Quahs solved their dinosaur pooh problem by shoveling all the pooh into one huge mound at the base of a cliff. On weekends and holidays, the male Pa'Quahs would climb up to the top of the cliff, and in a stunning display of male bravado, dive down in a terrifying freefall to land in the soft cushion of dinosaur dung at the bottom.

This impressed the women of the tribe to no end, and the man who dove deepest into the pile of shit usually won the hand of the woman with the largest breasts.

****

Mr. Matthews told his class that this original extreme sport was known as "Kaka Tooey," which is roughly translated as "Shit Diving."

****

In the time of the Pa'Quahs, man's best friend was not the dog. It was the compsognathus (see appendix). This is a scientific fact.

****

Karl and Arthur had both been taught in grade two geography that the center of the earth consisted of a solid metal called iron, and a viscous liquid called magma. The teachers who taught this had no idea whether or not it was really true. But they pretended that it was, and any child who disagreed was told that they were wrong.

This was typical of the school system at the time, teaching unimportant, useless facts based on the assumptions and best guesses of scientists and experts, rather than teaching more relevant, practical certainties of life, like how to be a good neighbor, how to act kindly towards others, or how to live simply and be content without living in a mansion and driving a shiny red sports car. These are things the schools *could* have been teaching instead of what kind of materials compose the earth's core.

Who really knows anyways? Maybe at the center of the earth there's neither solid iron nor liquid magma, but a single, small bumblebee whose buzzing wings provide the energy that makes the world go 'round. Sometimes the bumblebee buzzes too fast and sends out too much energy, causing the earth to shake and volcanoes to erupt. The only way the bumblebee will die is if it stops buzzing its wings. And the only way the bumblebee will stop buzzing its wings is if it dies.

And so the world keeps on turning.

Maybe we should teach kids nothing at all and let them sit around and think all day. Let them say that a circle has four corners. You can't tell them they're wrong. In their mind, a circle *does* have four corners.

Are you telling me that you think a circle has no corners at all? Well, you are perfectly correct, but so is little Jimmy when he says that a circle has 100 legs and lives on the planet Poopiter (between Jupiter and Saturn). A circle *does* have four corners, and it *is* perfectly round, and it *does* have 100 legs, and it *does* live on the planet Poopiter.

The imagination is *always* right.

****

Not to kick a dead cow, but imagine if school were to focus on questions like, "Given the choice, would you rather live your life in jail with full mental capacities, or live as a free man with only half of your mental capacities?"

"Would you rather be the greatest baseball player in the world but also be the world's hairiest man, or be the world's best opera singer but also be deprived of your sense of taste?"

"Would you rather have no facial features or no vocal chords?"

These types of questions require the full usage of a person's mental faculties: the imagination, a sense of empathy and compassion, and an ability to consider the big picture using logic and abstract thought.

These questions make us laugh, they make us reflect and consider, they make us really *think*. The discussions that result from these simple questions are almost always playful and fascinating, and inevitably end up in a deep exchange of social, philosophical, and thoroughly silly ideas.

Nobody cares what the square root of anything is. Nobody cares if you are capable of memorizing and regurgitating an entire passage of King Lear (unless of course, you are taking part in a play). Nobody cares who coined what term in what long-forgotten era. Dwelling on the meaningless and the mundane belittles our intelligence and stunts our imagination.

Of all the things we must mindfully, consistently utilize and cultivate in the learning process, imagination is the most important. Without a living, thriving imagination, a dull sheen slowly creeps in and covers everything you see, do, touch, taste, smell and hear.

It's a shame, then, that our schools do not put a greater focus on imagination. Why not teach classes that focus solely on using the imagination? "Imagination class." Students could share funny dreams, write short stories, listen to classical music, and generally be free to do anything they feel like doing, from creating art to walking in the forest, as long as it requires the active use of your imagination.

I know what you're thinking: it sounds like kindergarten. Well, what's wrong with kindergarten?

If a child escapes from the school system with a still-functioning imagination, with an imagination that is not broken and deformed, it is only because they fought life-and-limb to grasp it, and refused to let go. If a child escapes with a wild and vibrant imagination, it is truly a miracle and should be reported immediately to the person who handles miracles at your nearest Catholic Church.

Yes, in Karl and Arthur's time, school was essentially a means by which old, dull, imagionationless creatures stole the imaginations through the eyes, ears and mouths of those who were young and still had hope.

The bitter fruit told the sweet fruit how to grow. The corpses reached up from their dusty graves and whispered broken words of regret disguised as direction and advice into the ears of young fawns. The dead taught the living how to live and no one prospered.

****

A nice day at school:

Culture Class: students are taught about cultural relativity; not all people are the same; not all cultures are like ours; things are done differently all around the world; the options presented to you at birth are not your only options.

Thinking Class: students learn how to think for themselves; how to interpret messages around them; how to avoid worry and stress; students are taught about how little it matters what other people think of them; time allotted for silent thinking.

The History, Value, and Proper Usage of Money: students learn how to use money responsibly; the history of currency; the value of money; how to save; how to give; how money can be used for good and evil.

Imagination Class: students are encouraged to use their imaginations; emphasis on learning through creativity; only one rule: use your imagination.

Exploration Class: visit an interesting place you've never been before, and learn something new.

Art Class: learn to create things with your hands; learn to use your senses; learn to follow your instincts; learn to be intentionally playful, spontaneous and free.

Music Class: learn to play an instrument; try out as many instruments as you want; students create songs by stringing notes together that they think sound nice; collaborate with other students; perform a song for the class.

These last two are particularly important, as they instill in children life-long skills that ensure they will not grow up to become one of those people who is always saying, "I'm bored."

****

According to our logic, our logic makes the most sense.

****

I apologize for the rude interruption. Where are my manners?

****

"Unless there is a good reason for its being there, do not inject opinion into a piece of writing... Opinions scattered indiscriminately about leave the mark of egotism on a work." – E.B. White

CHAPTER 28

"Maybe I'm just a crazy lady who has wandered off the street and into this classroom and started explaining the mysteries of life to these young people. And they believe me, although I am utterly mistaken about simply everything." – *Kurt Vonnegut*

"If you want to become a friend of civilization,

then become an enemy of truth and a fanatic for harmless balderdash." – *Kurt Vonnegut*

"Others think we have to evolve, to become better monkeys with bigger brains. We don't need more information. We don't need bigger brains. All that is required is that we become less selfish than we are." – *Kurt Vonnegut*

"I stand before you today because I never stopped dawdling like an eight-year-old on a spring morning on his way to school. Anything can make me stop and look and wonder, and sometimes learn. I am a very happy man." – *Kurt Vonnegut*

****

"Where to?"

"Anywhere."

These were the only words exchanged between Sheila and the trucker since he had picked her up on the side of Turtle Pond Road.

The trucker farted. Sheila didn't know what to say.

"Bless you," she mumbled.

The trucker shot Sheila a sideways glance. "You know, the other day I came up with a way to categorize my farts." He paused. Perhaps he was thinking. Perhaps he was trying to create suspense. He continued, "I simply categorize my farts by what kind of animal they remind me of."

The trucker glanced over at Sheila. Behind his indiscriminate eyes, he was secretly hoping that Sheila would jump out of her seat in amazement and disbelief at his method of categorizing farts.

Sheila avoided the trucker's eyes, slightly embarrassed and doing her best to hide it.

The trucker waited, but Sheila said nothing. He cleared his throat and spit on the floor.

"So, for example," he said, "a really loud fart would be an elephant fart. A soft, peachy fart would be a panda bear fart. A weird sounding fart..." He scratched his head. "I guess a weird sounding fart would be a zebra fart or a platypus fart or something." Sheila could not believe what she was hearing.

"A deep, bassy fart would probably be a whale fart, or maybe a gorilla fart. A cute fart would be a koala bear fart, or maybe a kitten fart, depending on pitch. I still have to map it all out, iron out the wrinkles, you understand." The trucker excused himself sheepishly, ashamed of his half-finished system. He spoke as though having a conversation with a stranger about farts was as normal as talking about the weather. He wasn't finished yet.

"A funny fart would be a hyena fart," he chuckled. "A silent fart would be ah... hmm... Well I'm not sure what a silent fart would be... maybe a snake fart or a squirrel fart, or some kind of quiet animal like-"

"Okay! I get it!" Sheila blurted out a bit too loudly. Her face immediately blushed red, as the trucker turned and studied her reproachfully.

"I'm sorry." Sheila sighed. She didn't want the trucker to kick her out onto the side of the road.

"Your fart categories are very interesting," she said. "It's just that I'm tired, and I really need a few minutes to rest."

The trucker looked back at the road and straightened his orange meshed cap.

"Ten-four, little lady."

****

If you do not regard flatulence with at least a small degree of humour, then no matter what your age, you have lost some innate part of your sense of humour, and a small piece of the joy of life.

****

A white convertible swerved wildly down the street. Jim pulled into a donut shop parking lot, squealed to a stop, hopped out of the car and ran inside.

"I have to go pee," he told an old lady sitting by the front window. "Can you please watch my chariot for me? It's the white one with the big white horses strapped to it." He pointed out the window at the white convertible. Without waiting for the old lady to respond, Jim hurried off to the washroom.

While peeing, Jim thought he heard someone talking to him through the washroom door.

"I'm sorry," Jim yelled. "I can't hear you over the sound of my pee."

Jim zipped up his pants and emerged from the washroom to find that the old lady was no longer sitting at the table. He grumbled under his breath, something about how unreliable old people are, and walked towards the front door.

Jim stepped inside (outside) just in time to see his white chariot disappearing down the road in a cloud of dust, with a bob of gray hair poking up above the seat.

Jim's stolen car had just been re-stolen by an 86-year-old woman.

****

Sheila once wrote a short story about a calm, melancholy man who enjoyed going for quiet walks and observing the people around him. On most nights he would drink a cup of tea and read a book before going to bed. He mostly kept to himself.

But there was something different about this man, something that nobody else knew. Whenever the man heard strains of beautiful music, he would transform into an absolute maniac. He would break all the dishes in his cupboard, smash furniture, punch holes in the wall, jump up and down and rip out clumps of his hair.

As a result, the man had to make frequent trips to the store to buy new dishes and furniture. His hair was patchy and wild, with bits of dried blood here and there, along the hairline, behind the ears. The man's head looked like it had been attacked by a ferocious baby lion. People glanced at him strangely in the streets as he walked calmly by.

Then one day, while sitting in the train station, the man became acutely aware of the methodical tick-tick-ticking of the large clock on the wall. He tried to ignore the noise, but the ticking grew louder and louder.

The woman next to him began tapping her foot rhythmically on the tile floor. The wooden sole of her boot clicked in time with the clock.

The voices in the crowd seemed to swell in unison.

The wheels of a passing train clacked violently to an ancient tribal beat. Its steam whistle blared like an angry organ.

All these sounds blended together, embracing each other in mid-air. The man clenched his jaw and his hands began to tremble. His heart beat faster and his ears filled with a rush of beautiful static.

The sounds overwhelmed him and took over his senses. The man bolted up from his seat, ripped off his shoes and threw them at the clock, smashing the glass face, sending a shower of shards raining down upon the head of an angelic little girl. The man ripped off his shirt and swung it around in the air. He took a running start across the station floor, slung his shirt around a low-hanging pipe and swung himself feet-first through the plate-glass window.

He landed in the street, shirtless, bloody and barefooted like a wide-eyed jungle man. The sounds had disappeared, but his mind still swirled with heat and colour. He raced back home, locked the door behind him, dove into bed, and immediately fell into a deep slumber.

The man was awoken by a knock at his door. He didn't know how long he'd been asleep, maybe minutes, maybe hours. He got up and peeked through the window to see a police cruiser parked in front of his house. He quietly slid back under the sheets and lay motionless until the knocking at his door subsided. He peeked cautiously out the window and watched as two policemen got into the cruiser and drove away.

The man slipped into his pants and put on a new shirt. He hurried down the street to the doctor's office, where he pleaded with the doctor to cure him. He explained to the doctor that he didn't want to be thrown in jail, he didn't want to destroy things, and he didn't want to hurt anybody, but when the madness took over, when he heard lovely sounds blending together in defiant combinations and arrangements, he completely lost control of his mind and his actions.

The doctor thought for a moment, then reached into a drawer and handed the man a pair of earplugs. The man hesitated, pushed the earplugs into his ears, nodded to the doctor, and walked home.

From that day on, the man never acted like a maniac again. He kept the earplugs snugly in his ears day and night. He walked down the street and people smiled at him and tipped their hats. He lived the rest of his life without madness, starved of passion, unfamiliar with insanity, devoid of excitement.

He blended in perfectly with everybody else.

****

In a perfect world, every action and every movement is performed musically and rhythmically. There is no walking, but only dancing and shuffling and jumping and tapping. We all move together, striding down the sidewalk in unison, dancing in groups or with a partner, strolling through the markets arm-in-arm, moving our heads to the beat, a busy swarm of happiness.

Our conversations overlap with perfect timing and our words fit together in absolute harmony. We leave small intuitive pauses in between sentences before jumping back in, creating one giant song from many subtle melodies.

The birds chirp in harmony, brushing strokes of melody with their wings as the wind rustles through the willing leaves, compelling them to perform an impeccably timed crescendo.

Your heart races a metronome as your breath erupts in stochastic staccatos. A baby sneezes on the second beat and a door slams shut on the fourth. Rabbits jump at the sound of a child's laughter, and when a boy falls off his bike, the mountains beat their chests like echoing drums. The crickets take part in the ongoing celebration by performing a tiny bowed song for any participant who happens to walk by.

Small noises are no longer annoying or trivial, but are essential instruments playing important supporting roles, holding the entire structure together. You and I are not merely noisemakers, but we are metronomes for the world's song, we are conductors of the universe, and the universe is a song, and that song is life.

CHAPTER 29

"But they need to worry and betray time with urgencies false and otherwise, purely anxious and whiny, their souls really won't be at peace unless they can latch on to an established and proven worry and having once found it they assume facial expressions to fit and go with it, which is, you see, unhappiness, and all the time it all flies by them and they know it and that *too* worries them no end. Listen! Listen!" – *Jack Kerouac*

****

Karl was alone. He wore a blank expression on his face and it was difficult to tell if he was calm or agitated, content or distressed.

As Karl strolled through the center of Turtle Pond, he heard delicate strains of music escaping from a nearby alley. Karl followed the sounds into the alley to find a young boy standing by the wall, playing the violin.

The boy played with feeling, with certain delicateness, neither too loud nor too quiet. He wore nondescript clothing of a plain style. The boy was so unassuming that Karl was led to question whether he really existed, or if he was an angel, perhaps Michael's grandson, sent down from heaven to entertain him.

Karl stood mesmerized by the boy's playing, frozen in a wonderfully drawn out moment. After what seemed like an eternity, Karl took a few cautious steps forward, careful not to disturb the musician, and stopped a few paces away. A cat brushed up against Karl's leg, sweeping its stiff tail across his knee. It was then that Karl realized the alley was full of roaming cats, all apparently attracted by the strains of the boy's violin. Karl looked down to see a small clump of cats curled up at the boy's feet. The clump was purring and buzzing like one giant happy feline.

All at once the boy stopped playing. He looked up at Karl with a calm and violent fire in his eyes, a melancholy fire that burns because it must, and he said, "Strip away the music, and everything loses a little bit of life. Without music, this moment would not exist. You would not be here, and neither would I. This instrument, these strings, these notes bring us closer to the great mystery that lies at the heart of the universe. What music makes us feel is real. Music does not create fake or simulated emotions. It brings forth from within us all that is good and true." The boy paused and looked at Karl. Karl said nothing, but stared back, meeting the boy's gaze and not breaking it.

"Without music," the boy went on, "I would have stepped in front of a moving bus long ago." The boy let silence fill the air, and was not bothered by it.

"The beautiful thing about music is that you create your own joy. You create your own escape. You construct a place just as real as any other, and you are able to go there any time you want. *You* create that place. *You* create that escape, and you can shape it however you like. You can make that place beautiful, sad, joyful, content, *anything*. No matter what you build, you know that it is an honest place. When you go there, you feel alive, as though staring life in the face, no matter how dark or ugly it may appear to be."

The boy held up his violin and said, "This is my gun. A song is an emotional trigger. And music is the ammunition of life. If an existing song had never been written, the listeners would never be able to experience the combination of feelings that that song evoked. Music appears from nowhere, like a bullet from a sniper's rifle, and plunges into our hearts, granting us a moment of life that would be impossible to feel or achieve any other way. A song is an unnamable object, given as a gift to a person with open ears, whose privilege it is to translate it into the language of sound and music so that the rest of us can understand it."

"Without *Moonlight Sonata*, the world would be a different place. Millions of people would not know how it feels to listen to those beautiful notes, to let that song reach out and grab hold of their soul. A piece of humanity would be missing. But answer me this: was a piece of humanity missing before those notes flowed from Beethoven's fingers?"

Karl stood in silence. The boy was no longer a figment of his imagination, but was the only thing that was real. Karl was as hypnotized by the boy's words as he was by the music he had been playing on his violin.

"I like to imagine an angel wearing Mozart's hands for gloves," said the boy, and he smiled.

He placed his violin bow back onto the strings as if to play, then took it off again and lowered his violin back down. He furrowed his brow and breathed slowly.

"Music gives us a glimpse into the madness and ecstasy of God. If God *did* create the universe, he could not have done it without the aid of music, without being surrounded by and filled with music. Look around and see that the physical world contains the same joy and spontaneity that we find in music. Perhaps nature is a representation of the way music makes us feel. God heard a song and couldn't help but bring us into existence. Yes, *music made him do it*."

Then the boy told Karl a story: "In the beginning was Music. Music gave birth to a beautiful being. That beautiful being heard the Music and was filled with energy. The beautiful being summoned his Musical energy and created the universe in a furious rush of movement and motion. With a few sweeps of his arms he flung the stars far and wide. He flicked his wrist and sent the planets spinning into eternity. Laughing and dancing, the being plunged his hands deep inside the Music and pulled out one wonderful object after another. With each object he pulled out, the being jumped and shouted with childish delight."

"That original Music gave birth to the original being, and that beautiful being was inspired by the Music to create the universe, and the universe has acted as the inspiration for all Music created ever since. Why do we find music so mysterious? Perhaps it is because we recognize our birth within it."

CHAPTER 30

"To try to imagine what animals could praise in us" - *Elias Canetti*

****

"My cousin Jeffrey is a manager in Paxton," said the trucker. "I'm sure he'd be happy to set you up with a job. Cousin Jeffrey is always looking for new employees."

"Oh that would be wonderful!" Sheila's face lit up, then her smile faded slightly as another thought occurred to her. "And what kind of work does your cousin Jeffrey do?"

"Oh, this and that," the trucker looked at Sheila and grinned. It was getting dark outside and the shadows cast a sinister line across his face. "Don't you worry, little lady. We'll take good care of you." He rolled down his window and spit into the wind.

****

Arthur slept soundly in the back of the truck, like only an amnesiac could. After many hours had passed, Arthur suddenly awoke. He was startled and disoriented. He sneezed five times. He lifted his head from the pile of hay and manure that was his makeshift pillow. He scratched his right cheek and yawned.

The trailer was pitch black except for a few rays of dusty sunlight shining in through the cracks and holes in the trailer's side. Though Arthur didn't know where he was, he was not worried or scared at all. Sure, it was dark in the back of the truck, and the ride was pretty bumpy, but one place was as good as another.

The sound of a man's laughter echoed through the metal siding. It was followed by the sound of a woman's voice. Arthur sat up and listened. He thought he recognized the woman's voice, but he couldn't be sure.

Propping himself up on one elbow, Arthur leaned over and placed his ear against the front wall of the trailer. He strained to hear the female voice above the banging and rattling of the moving truck. He caught a jumbled sentence here and there, but could not make out what the voice was saying.

Arthur was sure he recognized the woman's voice. But who was she? How did he know her? Arthur listened for two more minutes, but heard nothing more. The voices had stopped. Arthur plopped back down onto the pile of hay and fell asleep with a heavy sigh, not knowing who he was, or where he was going.

****

"Excuse me," said Jim. "My chariot has just been stolen from your parking lot."

The waitress finished folding a stained tablecloth and looked up at Jim. "Would you like me to call the police?" she asked.

"No!" blurted Jim. "I mean, certainly not! I mean, no thank you. I wouldn't want to disturb the local police with such a petty matter." Jim looked around nervously and tapped his fingertips on the counter. "But I do have one small favor to ask," said Jim. "Can you tell me how far it is to Paxton from here?"

The waitress chomped on her gum and studied Jim's face suspiciously. Jim's heart sank. Had he been going in the wrong direction this entire time? Was Paxton now a thousand miles away?

The waitress reached under the counter and pulled out a menu. She slid the menu across the counter and placed her finger at the top.

Jim looked down and read the title out loud, "Paxton Diner."

"Sir," said the waitress. "Welcome to Paxton."

Jim's eyes lit up like fireflies.

****

The brakes squealed and Sheila jerked awake. She sat up in the warm, padded passenger seat and rubbed her eyes with the backs of her knuckles.

"Here we are," said the trucker. "Paxton." In an unexpected gesture that was extremely elegant for a truck driver, he swept his arm through the air with a flourish, as if welcoming Sheila to a private tropical island.

Sheila peered out the window and could barely make out the dim outlines of a few angular buildings through the darkness.

The trucker noticed Sheila's apprehensive expression and smiled. "I called ahead to my cousin Jeffrey while you were sleeping," he said. "He'll be expecting you."

Sheila squinted out the window, studying the looming silhouette of the nearest building. "Well, I guess I should be going then," said

Sheila. She turned to face the trucker and presented him with the most grateful, gracious smile her tired face could muster under the circumstances. "Thanks for everything," she said.

The trucker tipped his hat and nodded. Sheila stepped down to the pavement and slammed the door behind her. As she walked down the path towards the nearest building she heard the passenger door swing open behind her.

"Hey," the truckers voice rang out through the still night air. Sheila turned around slowly to face him. The trucker was leaning all the way across the front seat with his arm stretched out just far enough to hold open the passenger door. Sheila readied herself for anything: an invitation to dinner, an invitation to his trailer park, a marriage proposal.

"I was just wondering," said the trucker, smiling sheepishly, "if I could pick your brain really quick before we part ways." He stared down at Sheila with his big blue trucker eyes full of dust and wise love, and for a split second Sheila found herself attracted to this dirty man with his puffy cheeks and boyish features. Their eyes locked, Sheila bashfully batted her lashes, and for a moment these two misfit vagabonds were transported from a deserted dirt road to a glossy Hollywood screen with hundreds of spectators all watching and holding their collective breath. Just for one short moment.

"I wanted to ask you," said the trucker. "What do you think the funniest animal fart would be?" The trucker broke the Hollywood magic, and Sheila was rapidly whisked back to reality. She stood in utter shock.

"I mean the funniest animal fart of them all," the trucker went on. "What animal do you think it would be?" He paused and looked at Sheila with wide eyes, waiting for an answer, hoping for the best. Sheila's jaw hung open and did not move. Slightly disappointed, the trucker was forced to answer his own question.

"I always thought a rabbit fart would be pretty funny," he said. "Can you imagine a farting rabbit? All cute and innocent and furry, just sitting there. You'd never expect a rabbit to fart." He chuckled and pulled himself across to the passenger seat. "I think a rabbit that fartcd every time it jumped would be pretty funny, don't you?"

Sheila's mind had frozen somewhere between fear and disbelief. The trucker went on, oblivious to the fact that he had shocked his audience into silence.

"I think a horse fart would be pretty funny too. Can you imagine that?" He bent his wrist and flapped his hand in the air, doing his best imitation of a horse's tail blowing in the wind. He laughed and slapped his hand on the seat. He stared at Sheila for a few seconds, not knowing what to make of this strange woman who was so unresponsive to his jokes.

"All right, little lady," said the trucker. "You take care of yourself." He had nothing more to say. He closed the door and pulled away.

A small, shadowy figure scuttled away from the spot where the truck had just been pulled over. The figure swiveled its head around and disappeared into the shadows.

Oblivious to the shadowy figure just a few

192

steps behind her, Sheila squinted up at the sign hanging above the door of the dark grey building where Cousin Jeffrey was apparently a manager. The sign read, in black, menacing letters, "Paxton County Prison."

****

Sheila once wrote a short story about a world where people greeted each other by saying, "Hello, what is your yearly income?" People would respond to this greeting by stating their yearly income and then inquiring about the first person's yearly income.

"Hello, my yearly income is thirty-thousand dollars. What is *your* yearly income?"

Whichever person was found to have the lowest yearly income had to immediately do twenty-five jumping jacks, compliment the other person's clothing, and make them a roast beef sandwich. In the event of a tie, each person had to rent a sailboat for the other person's grandmother for one weekend in July. If the other person's grandmother was dead, the person had the option to either re-shingle their roof or buy them a new set of golf clubs.

Sheila was forced to stop writing this short story before it was finished because she was repulsed by roast beef sandwiches.

****

If you are over the age of 20, and you still believe that money and fame are important, close this book immediately, toss an apple high into the air and let it fall on your head.

****

"Security is the opposite of freedom," says the homeless man to the millionaire.

****

The sun stretched its long golden fingers above the horizon as Arthur wandered through the sleepy streets of Paxton. The sky was hazy grey and full of lazy clouds.

Arthur had lost a shoe somewhere in the back of the truck and he now kicked off his other shoe to even things out. Balancing on one foot and then the other, Arthur ripped off his socks and continued down the oil-stained street in bare feet.

He saw a large rock about the size of a watermelon sitting beneath a tree. The rock wasn't doing anything. It was just sitting there. Arthur felt magnetically drawn towards it. He approached the rock slowly, with growing anticipation. When he was a couple feet away, he suddenly pounced on the rock and threw it aside with both hands. Arthur looked at the ground where the rock had been sitting, but there was nothing there. There were no clues. There was no treasure. There was nothing.

****

A few minutes later, the sun was showing its entire naked body above the horizon. The sun flashed the earth and was not ashamed.

Arthur was meandering through a field

behind an old rundown factory when he stumbled upon a group of people who were all standing in a circle and laughing loudly. Arthur stood and watched them for a while, trying to figure out what they could possibly be laughing about. All Arthur could see was a field and a factory and some trees, and there was nothing very funny about any of those things.

Arthur walked into the middle of the circle and gazed at the hysterical faces around him. Some people were doubled over, holding their stomachs and gasping for air.

"Why are you laughing?" Arthur asked no one in particular.

"Because it makes us feel happy," a woman called out between gasps.

Arthur stood for a while longer, watching all the laughing people. Their laughter rang through the air, sounding strange among the trees and the grass where silence usually reigns.

Arthur took a sharp breath and tried to force out a laugh, "Hhhaaaaah." It sounded hollow and contrived.

"How do I do it?" asked Arthur. "How do I laugh like you guys are laughing?"

No one responded this time. Everyone was too busy laughing. Arthur tried to laugh again. He laughed for a few seconds and smiled slightly, but his laughter still sounded foreign to his ears, hollow, sad and slightly sinister. Arthur felt a tingling sensation behind his ears. It felt refreshing, but Arthur still didn't know who he was.

CHAPTER 31

"I call him Joe because he calls me Joe. When Carl is with us he is Joe too. Everybody is Joe because it's easier that way. It's also a pleasant reminder not to take yourself too seriously." – *Henry Miller*

****

It was pouring rain in Paxton, and Jim was standing on the sidewalk shampooing his head. Brown suds ran down his arms and dripped off his elbows. His eyes were closed and he was whistling a melody that resembled the warbling song of a drowning bird. Jim was soaked from head to toe. He was in heaven.

Jim had just returned from Vivacious Vincenzo's Shampoo Emporium where he had convinced a kind lady to buy him a bottle of Vivacious Vincenzo's Shampoo Formula For Men, and had put another 30 bottles on hold after promising the cashier he would return to pick them up within the next two days. Jim didn't know where he'd get the money, but he knew he wouldn't leave Paxton until those 30 bottles of shampoo were in his possession. He hadn't traveled all this way for nothing.

Jim didn't see the two police officers approaching him. One officer was tall and male, and the other was short and female. Neither of them looked very pleased to be inside (outside) in the pouring rain. As the officers walked towards Jim, Tall Officer cleared his throat loudly. Jim didn't hear him. There was shampoo in his ears. Tall Officer tapped Jim on the shoulder and Jim's eyes popped open.

"Hello," Jim smiled at them. He closed his eyes and continued massaging his head.

The officers exchanged an annoyed look. Tall Officer tapped Jim on the shoulder harder this time, with two firm fingers. Jim wiped the suds away from his eyes and smiled at the officers again. They didn't smile back.

"Sir," said Tall Officer. "You can't be doing that here."

"Really?" said Jim. "Why not?" Jim's confusion was genuine but the officers mistook his silly smile for a sarcastic grin.

Short Female Officer felt a surge of manly courage and piped up, "Don't get smart with us, buddy."

Jim squirted a generous heap of shampoo onto the crown of his head and placed the bottle back on the ground. He ignored the officers and vigorously rubbed the shampoo until it formed a wild, bubbly afro on top of his head.

"Do you want us to arrest you, sir?" Short Female Officer took another step forward.

Tall Officer looked down at Short Female Officer and frowned. ,"Calm down, Fran," he said.

Short Female Officer's chest deflated a little and she took a step back.

"Sir," said Tall Officer. "I'm going to have to ask you to put down the shampoo bottle and cease what you're doing."

Jim's ears were full of fresh shampoo and his mind was a hundred miles away.

Short Female Officer scowled. She stepped forward and grabbed Jim's wrist.

"Hey," said Jim. He tried to pull away, but Short Female Officer only tightened her grip. Jim panicked and tried to jerk his wrist away harder. He was suddenly frantically afraid that the officers were trying to steal his shampoo. Thinking fast, Jim shook his head back and forth like a shaggy dog, sending stinging suds into Short Female Officer's eyes. Short Female Officer yelped and let go of Jim's wrist.

A few moments later, a group of surprised Paxton citizens watched as a ragged, bearded man ran wildly down the street with two cops in tow, clutching a bottle of shampoo like a starving man grasping a stolen loaf of bread, with clouds of bubbles trailing behind his head like wisps of magic.

****

Female cops would grow mustaches if they could.

****

The entire town of Turtle Pond was gathered inside the school gymnasium, packed tightly together like fish in a mailbox. The last time there was such a large gathering in Turtle Pond was when Reynold Reynoldson had broken two Guinness World Records in one day.

Spanning the front wall was a colorful banner that read, "Permanium Awareness Week Closing Ceremonies."

The crowd sat in nervous anticipation. The ceremonies were about to begin. Mayor Cotton had announced the previous morning that there would be a special guest in attendance, and word had quickly spread around town that it might be Reynold Reynoldson.

Mayor Cotton strolled out onto stage amid raucous applause and chants of, "*Caw-tin, Caw-tin.*" Permanium Awareness Week had done wonders for Mayor Cotton's popularity.

The crowd quieted down as Mayor Cotton stepped up to the microphone. He was wearing a grey and red train conductor's hat. He puffed out his chest in an effort to appear important and mayoral.

"First of all," Mayor Cotton began. "I can't tell you, *all* of you, how proud I am of your courage, your strength, and your spirit."

Wild applause.

"This past week, our small town of Turtle Pond has come together as one big family to show our support for permaniums."

Wild applause.

"I believe we've sent a message to the world that it is no longer okay to discriminate, to hate, or to make fun of permaniums."

Wild applause, three loud whistles, assorted hooting and hollering.

Someone in the back of the crowd started chanting, "*Rey-nold, Rey-nold.*" Others quickly followed suit, until the entire crowd was chanting together, "*REY-NOLD, REY-NOLD.*"

"Alright, alright." Mayor Cotton chuckled. "Without further ado, I'd like to present tonight's guest of honour, the man to whom this entire week has been dedicated..." He paused for dramatic effect and swept his hands towards the side curtain. "Reynold Reynoldson!"

The crowd jumped to their feet and yelled

their heads off. Reynold didn't come out. They yelled some more.

"Come on out Reynold!" Mayor Cotton yelled. He waited a long moment, and then walked behind the curtain.

The crowd yelled and whistled. They clapped and clapped, but Reynold didn't come out. People began to look at their neighbors and shrug their shoulders.

Here's the thing: No one had actually checked to see if Reynold Reynoldson had accepted his invitation to the ceremony. They had just assumed he would come. Nobody knew that Reynold Reynoldson was currently eating a salted pretzel while taking a dip in a hotel Jacuzzi over 2,000 miles away.

As the crowd fell quieter and quieter, a young boy wandered out onto the empty stage from behind one of the red velvet curtains. It was Karl. No one made a move to stop Karl as he approached the microphone. Karl calmly lowered the microphone to the right height, and the audience grew silent.

Karl scanned the audience with fierce eyes that did not belong to him. He opened his mouth and a torrent of words burst forth like water breaking through a dam.

"I stand before you today, pure and innocent," said Karl. "I do not claim to know anything. I have filled myself up with your collective wisdom, and still I am empty. I have listened to you speak, and have learned nothing."

The people were confused. Where had Mayor Cotton gone? Where was Reynold Reynoldson? Why was this boy speaking into the microphone? What was he saying?

"Who here can actually tell me what a permanium is?" Karl scanned the crowd. Somewhere a starving eagle was hunting with a little boy's eyes. "It's great that you support a cause, but you should never believe so strongly in an idea without first knowing exactly what it is that you believe in. Some of you have good hearts, but most of you are just dumb." The crowd shifted uneasily.

"I've learned that people cannot answer your questions. The answer to every question can be found in one place: Music." Karl closed his eyes and listened to the boy playing the violin down the street. No one else could hear it.

"The answers are all around you. Everywhere you look, everything you touch, everything you hear is music. Music is contained inside you and exists all around you."

"The last few days I have stumbled on a few things that I now hold to be true. First, you must get rid of the ego. It is nothing but trouble. Throw your ego out the window. Always remember that it is a noble act to hold the door open for others. Next time you want something and someone else wants it too, let them have it. They need it more than you do. Promote strangers to friends, men to brothers and women to sisters. Try on a different pair of shoes every day. Reconsider your reflex to swat at living things. To have an imagination is not childish, but to *not* have an imagination is adultish. If you ask yourself every time before you speak, 'Is it worth it?' and only proceed when the answer is 'yes,' you'll find you'll rarely ever speak again. Spread rumors through your silence and not through your words. Always follow the curious urges of the imagination. Get rid of the ego. Please, throw the ego out the window. One day you'll thank me for this, and the whole world will thank you in return."

Karl turned to leave, hesitated, and stepped back to the microphone.

"And stop pretending to know things you don't. It makes things very confusing for us children."

With that, Karl walked off the stage and was gone. The crowd sat still, like a classroom of schoolboys frozen with guilt. The silence was so loud it would have hurt the ears of a deaf person, had one been present.

Then a strange thing happened. Another boy, slightly younger than Karl, wandered out onto the stage and approached the microphone. He cleared his throat and began to burp the alphabet. Mayor Cotton wandered back out from behind the curtain, unaware of what had just taken place.

"Get off the stage, you rotten brat!" he yelled at the boy. The boy burst into tears and ran away.

****

A few blocks away, a gentle light illuminated an alley full of cats. The violin boy was gone, but a bundle of interwoven words now bounced off the walls where he had stood. The cats purred as the words were invisibly spoken by a voice so quiet you could only hear it if you closed your eyes: "I want to preserve your heart in a jar and throw it to the bottom of the ocean, so that when humanity fails in a million years, they'll have a shining example of where to begin again."

****

All the little things, the earnest, the sincere, the naïve parts of ourselves we leave behind because they are childish and time-consuming.

CHAPTER 32

"To hell with reality! I want to die in music, not in reason or in prose. People don't deserve the restraint we show by not going into delirium in front of them. To hell with them!" – *Louis-Ferdinand Celine*

****

Arthur left the laughing people in the field, and walked across Paxton's main street. He was not sure where he was going, but as long as he kept walking he didn't care.

Arthur peered through the front window of a coffee shop and saw a man throwing his cup of coffee onto the floor. The man yelled something at the waitress, spit on the ground, and stormed inside (outside), brushing past Arthur as he went.

The man was angry because his coffee had

been served in a Styrofoam cup. How dare they serve him coffee in a Styrofoam cup! Everybody knows that Styrofoam is like poison for the environment.

Imagine that. A man who is trying to save the earth for future generations forgets to be kind to those who are on the earth right now. There is a kind of humanist that I call a "futurist humanist," which is a person that is only kind to people who do not yet exist.

Arthur walked down the street, passing the city limits. "Hahahgch," he tried to laugh again, but choked on his spit. He found a dirt path and followed it into a forest.

****

Here is one of the prominent problems in the world: People take things personally. People get offended. This causes problems. You cannot take anything personally. You cannot be offended. You cannot be hurt. None of these things are possible. You are human and so is everybody else. There is nothing anybody can do that you cannot understand, and if you understand something, then you cannot be hurt by it. Be the duck's oily feathers. Take nothing personally, and you will live freely like a fish swimming down a clear river.

****

"For the last time, no you *cannot* have your shampoo back." The prison guard was becoming impatient.

Jim stopped pacing his cell and sat down

on the hard steel bench. He held his hands in front of his face and tried to stop them from shaking. He reached down and vigorously scratched his left ankle. Jim's skin was itchy all over, and he could feel his heart beating like a hammer in his chest. A bead of sweat dripped off his forehead and landed on his arm, creating a clean splotch of skin within a patch of dirt, like a reverse birthmark.

Jim longed for his shampoo. He *needed* it. He was going mad without it. He was being tortured by a thousand tiny creatures, patiently working their way into all of his pores and holes and crevices. It had only been 8 hours since he shampooed his head with Vivacious Vincenzo's Special Shampoo Formula For Men, and already he was sinking deep into the first stages of withdrawal. Jim closed his eyes and clenched his jaw. He didn't know how much longer he could survive.

****

Though there were three other empty cells in Paxton prison, the guards had thrown their only two prisoners together into one cell, like little boys throwing a spider and an earwig into a plastic bottle in hopes that they'll fight each other.

Jim's cellmate was a man named Drunk Andrew. He was Groggy Gary's cousin. Drunk Andrew had been an amateur boxer in his teenage years. He used to get neighborhood kids to throw bricks at him to make him quicker and lighter on his feet. Drunk Andrew would deftly dodge the bricks and playfully taunt the kids, saying, "Hah! Is that all you got?"

Then one day, a kid's father threw a brick at Drunk Andrew when he wasn't looking. The brick smashed into the back of Drunk Andrew's head. He was hospitalized for three months, and the doctors told him he could never box again. Drunk Andrew did his best to recover from this terrible blow to the head, but he soon realized that he would never fully recover, and would never be able to box again. So instead of boxing and working out, Drunk Andrew began to get drunk every day. It wasn't long before Drunk Andrew lost his home, and took up drinking full time. Strangely, Drunk Andrew picked up his nickname long before he actually became an alcoholic, due to his unique, off-kilter boxing style. Fate has an excellent sense of humor.

****

Jim was unaware that Drunk Andrew was also going through a withdrawal. Drunk Andrew had consumed copious amounts of whiskey, gin, moonshine, and whatever other toxic substances he could get his hands on, every single day for the last three years. His impressive drinking streak had come to an anti-climactic end three days ago, when the police caught him drinking gin from a hotdog vendor's shoe. It wouldn't have been a problem if the hotdog vendor hadn't still been wearing his shoe at the time.

Now, for the first time in over two years, Drunk Andrew was experiencing reality, bare and raw. Terrible! Horrifying! Refreshing! Drunk

Andrew was overwhelmed by a savage clearheadedness that took his body by storm.

The uneducated reader may not be aware that past scientific studies have attempted to prove the existence of a reciprocal relationship taking place in the space between sanity and insanity. Scientists have attempted to prove that the experience of a sane person turning insane is identical to the experience of an insane person turning sane. Scientists have also drawn the same parallel between the experiences of a sober person becoming an alcoholic, and vice-versa. One scientist was quoted as saying, "It's all a matter of perspective," and then laughing maniacally and jumping off a bridge.

****

One such study was performed by Dr. Yousef Diaborak of Russia, in the early 1950s. Dr. Diaborak's study explored the effects of alcohol on a group of 20 perfectly normal, healthy gorillas. Dr. Diaborak began his study by administering 6 ounces of alcohol daily to each gorilla. The alcohol was administered through large metal tubes inserted through the bars of the cage. Dr. Diaborak gradually increased the amount of alcohol every two weeks for one full year. By the end of the year, the gorillas were consuming nearly 70 ounces of hard alcohol each day.

I should mention that before the study began, Dr. Diaborak performed a series of blind taste tests with the gorillas to see which type of alcohol they enjoyed most. He imported all sorts of exotic beers and colorful liquors from all corners of the earth. There was Toucan Fire Breath Rum from Northern India, which was said to turn the inner walls of your stomach into a fluorescent rainbow after you drank it, though this had never been proven. There was Fatty Grey Zambooka from deep in the jungles of the African Congo, which was filtered a hundred times through the intestines of a sacred tribe of elephants, one elephant at a time. There was Russian Man Vodka, which was distilled by a drunk Russian who threw in whatever ingredients he could find lying around the house. In the end, it was discovered that the gorillas favored the cheap rum that Dr. Diaborak picked up at the corner store for a pocketful of change.

Now before you jump to conclusions and claim that Dr. Diaborak's experiments qualified as animal abuse, you should know that the gorillas were treated extremely well, practically like royalty. They lived in a caged palace, complete with banana trees, jungle gym, dining room, human butlers, kitchen with six fridges, and a 20-foot television screen that played nothing but Charlie Chaplin movies all day (gorillas love Charlie Chaplin!). To top it all off, Dr. Diaborak brought in a team of geo-architects to build a rushing river powered by 32 pumps that pushed torrents of water down a flowing waterfall, emptying into a sandy pond where the gorillas drank and splashed around every morning.

****

Dr. Diaborak's experiment ended tragically. The drunken gorillas had been pressuring him nearly every day, urging him to join in on their drunken games and wrestling matches. Dr. Diaborak had been able to resist for a number of months, but eventually he couldn't stand the taunts anymore. He gave in, and joined the gorillas for one drink inside their cage. He left immediately after finishing his drink. But the next day, he entered the cage again to drink with the gorillas. This time, one drink led to another, and another, and another, and before Dr. Diaborak knew it, he was partaking in naked wrestling matches with the gorillas, smearing mud on his face, and rubbing banana peels under his armpits.

****

Dr. Diaborak's body was discovered by the police five months later, laying face-down on the sandy bank of the wading pool. The cage door was swung open and the gorillas were nowhere to be seen. The police found Dr. Diaborak's journal lying open on his desk. The journal entry for Monday March 15th read: "Today I joined the gorillas for a drink. I wanted to immerse myself in their environment, to get a firsthand understanding of how they live... It was interesting."

Four days later, on Thursday, March 18th, Dr. Diaborak had made the following journal entry, which would be his last: "I have never had so much fun in my life. Gorillas are awesome!"

****

One gorilla named Artikus turned up in Times Square several months later. Traces of Dr. Diaborak's blood were found in his hair. The other 19 gorillas were never found. The fateful events that led to Dr. Diaborak's death remain unknown.

****

Needless to say, the results of the study were inconclusive.

CHAPTER 33

"Oh brother what a life that was! Into the graves with us." - *Christoph Meckel*

****

Drunk Andrew was sober. The sponge in his head had been squeezed dry of alcohol. He was slowly becoming sane again. His mind was clearing. Bad ideas and unqualified beliefs were being chopped down like trees. Misconceptions and untruths were being ripped out of the corners of his mind like cobwebs on cleaning day.

****

The path opened up into a clearing of ferns and brush. Arthur could see a deer's white tail dancing above the bright tips of the tall grass. The sun created a halo of white light around the edge of the clearing. Arthur walked between two trees and entered the clearing.

****

Sheila was in luck. Paxton County Prison was in need of a new guard. Cousin Jeffrey handed Sheila a uniform and told her to report for her first shift in ten minutes. The prison consisted of four holding cells, a bathroom, a break room and a cramped office.

****

Karl left the assembly and passed through the doors of Turtle Pond School for the last time. He burst inside (outside) and began walking with no destination in mind. He walked and walked and didn't know where he was going, but he felt strangely drawn to continue walking. All he was sure of was that he didn't feel like going home.

****

Drunk Andrew's mind didn't know what to do with its sudden freedom, and so it reacted in the same way a stomach reacts when it experiences shock: it instinctively expelled its semi-decomposed contents in violent fashion.

****

Arthur sat on a log and looked around. He looked at the green grass, the red and purple flowers, the white deer tail, the golden-yellow bird, the brown twigs and branches, the orange chipmunk, and the pink and blue sky. He said to himself, "How could anyone ever *possibly* choose a favourite colour?"

****

Sheila locked herself in the bathroom and quickly changed into her new uniform. She opened the door to see Cousin Jeffrey putting on his jacket, getting ready to leave. Sheila's jaw dropped. On her very first shift, Sheila was going to be left alone to look after the prison.

****

Karl stopped in front of an old barn. One half of the roof was caved in and many parts of the walls were rotted out or missing altogether. Karl climbed up the splintered wooden ladder and lay down in the hayloft. He stared up at the blue sky through a hole in the roof.

****

Jim's cellmate had transformed into a lucid madman. Drunk Andrew paced back and forth from wall to wall, like a caged lion at feeding time. He opened his mouth and shouted, "I want to know more than anyone has ever known before. I want to laugh and cry and be genuinely surprised, and know what it feels like to die and be brought back to life!"

****

Arthur looked around and jumped in surprise. A massive moose stood just a few feet behind him. How long had it been standing there watching him?

****

"We've got a couple of real crazies locked up right now," called Cousin Jeffrey from the doorway.

Sheila cleared her throat nervously, and nodded her head.

"They just came in last night," said Cousin Jeffrey. "They're in cell four if you'd like to go take a look. Nothing much to look at though." He grunted goodnight and walked inside (outside), leaving Sheila all alone in the dead-silent prison.

****

Karl stared through a gaping hole in the roof of the barn, and thought about nothing at all. After he finished thinking about nothing, he thought about how much he loved the colour of the sky, how if you follow it down vertically from the top, you can pick out a million different shades of blue, each one just as lovely as the next.

****

"I want to know which is better, life or death?" Drunk Andrew yelled. "And is death really death if you go on to live again? Or is death just a moment? A meaningless, unimportant moment that doesn't deserve a fraction of the attention it gets..."

****

The moose was staring at Arthur with big black marble eyes, peering deep into his soul, asking him silent questions, and daring Arthur to answer. The moose snorted and flicked his ear. Arthur laughed.

****

The prison was silent except for the occasional echo of tiny scurrying feet from somewhere unseen. Sheila looked out the window and watched Cousin Jeffrey's pickup truck pull away. She was alone in a strange prison with two crazy prisoners. She looked down to see that her hands were trembling.

****

While Karl was admiring blue shade #230,458, a soft voice glided through the cracks in the walls and floated to his ears. It was a haunting voice singing somewhere in the distance. It was a kind wind that carried the voice to Karl.

****

Drunk Andrew gestured wildly with his hands,

swinging his arms in wide arcs and circles. "I want to know it all!" he yelled.

Jim groaned and clutched his chest.

"Why 'I' and not 'S?' Why 'face' and not 'tree?'" The lucid wildcat grabbed Jim's lifeless shoulders and shook him violently.

Jim responded with a pitiful groan. Drunk Andrew let go of his hold, as Jim began to convulse.

****

Arthur laughed and it sounded true and pure. Childish laughter. Bounding laughter. It bounced off the trees. It did not sound strange. It belonged there, in the forest, with the moose and the trees.

****

Dirty magazines and dirty dishes were strewn across the break room table. Muddy boots and tattered clothing decorated the floor. A sandwich crust was growing mold in the corner. Sheila shook her head in disgust.

****

Karl climbed down the broken ladder, skipped over the smile at the bottom, and began walking across the endless field, toward the singing voice. As the voice grew louder, it also grew more haunting. It bit into Karl. It hit him in the face and made him smile.

****

"Tell me everything that no one has ever known. Why this and not that? Why are things the way they are? Tell me now!" Drunk Andrew was in a rage. His soberness had made him drunk with reality. He lifted Jim's limp body up off the bench and threw him to the concrete floor.

****

Arthur caught himself laughing. Something about the trees and the tall grass and the deer's tail and the silly moose made him laugh. He smiled and he laughed. Yes, he was happy.

****

There was a foreign green substance, perhaps soup, in a bowl in the break room fridge, and a 6-pack of pop with three cans gone. The cupboards were mostly empty except for some broken plastic dishes, and tiny pellets of mouse poop. Sheila flicked off the light and walked toward the office.

****

A dark figure lay in the middle of the field. Brown and green trees were scattered around him like wooden sentinels. Karl came closer, and recognized the man's face. It was Groggy Gary. He was singing.

****

"What is known is but one tiny grain of sand on

the vast beach of the unknown. Were it to be reversed your mind would explode." Drunk Andrew stopped pacing for a moment, and looked down at Jim's motionless body with pity in his eyes.

****

Arthur listened to the sound of his own laughter. He heard something familiar in it. He recognized it as his own.

****

The filing cabinet contained papers that looked like they would disintegrate if Sheila touched them. She blew the dust off the lid of a cardboard box, and opened it up. It was full of mousetraps.

****

Groggy Gary rested in a patch of dandelions. His black shirt was dirty and torn. His pants had only one leg. The other leg was floating in a river somewhere. His nose was crooked. His mouth was sideways. His beard was a tangled ball of yarn. His eyes shone through the dirt on his face. He sang:

If I should ever die,
The last words from my lips
Will be "Thank you to whomever
Created all of this."

****

"But what good is it to know everything? The knowledge would wrap like rope around my wrists. My thoughts would become a noose around my neck. I would never move again. I would sit on this bench all day." Drunk Andrew sat down on the bench and put his head in his hands. "If I knew *everything*, would I be *happy*? Would I be *sad*? Would it even make a *difference*? I would know everything about happiness, and everything about sadness, and I wouldn't have to feel them to know how they feel. I would never have to *feel* again. I would know how feelings feel better than anyone could feel how they feel." Drunk Andrew's mind was pushing fearlessly forward, struggling to make up for years of lost time.

****

The moose stood still and flicked its ears. The birds sang, and the forest breathed. Arthur laughed again. He couldn't help it. And then, suddenly, he felt his memory come rushing back. His eyes brightened, and he shot up from the log. The moose looked at him cautiously.

****

An agitated voice came echoing down the hallway. Sheila hoped the prisoners weren't fighting. She didn't want to have to deal with any problems. She wouldn't know what to do.

****

Karl lay down in the dandelions next to Groggy Gary, and closed his eyes. He sang along:

And if I should live forever,
I'll utter those same words,
But I'll sing them every day
To the trees and to the birds.

****

"I would know what wise is, and I would know how to be it. I would know how little you know, and I would know how to laugh at you in just the right tone to make the tears burst forth." Drunk Andrew was on the verge of eruption. His eyes bulged, and sweat streamed down his face. "I would know how to *do* anything, and *say* anything, and *think* anything, and *be* anything. I would know how little I used to know, how small, how stupid, how proud, how thoughtless I was, before I knew everything, as I spoke these words." Drunk Andrew fell silent. He was completely drained. He had nothing more to say. He could not move or think or speak. Jim groaned, and his arm twitched.

****

Arthur ran and jumped through the forest. He laughed loudly and freely. His laughter echoed off the wise tree trunks, and flooded back into his ears. "I remember who I am!" he yelled.

From somewhere deep in the forest came the sound of a moose laughing.

****

The voice had stopped yelling, but Sheila thought she should check up on the prisoners anyway. It was her job, after all. She turned off the office light, and closed the door behind her.

****

As Groggy Gary continued to sing, Karl opened his eyes and stared up at blue shade #18,004. He realized that he did not need to close his eyes to be happy. He could look at the things around him, and make them move. He could mold physical things with his imagination. No longer were all the wild and wonderful visions trapped inside his head. He could take out his ideas and spread them like a thin layer of stained glass over the earth. He could keep his eyes wide open without having his pupils stung by what he saw. He could look at reality without being repulsed, because he could change what he saw.

****

Drunk Andrew summoned his last ounce of energy, and dragged Jim's sweat-soaked body up onto the bench. Jim could not hold up his own weight. He slid off the bench and fell back to the floor. Drunk Andrew lay down beside Jim and closed his eyes. He sighed like a horse. "Oh, I've wasted so much time..."

****

"...My life is short, but it will matter," said

Drunk Andrew. He turned his head and looked at Jim. Jim's mouth hung open. He was no longer breathing. "It will matter," Drunk Andrew repeated. "It will matter... It will matter... It will matter... It will matter... It......"

****

Every dead person is like every other one.

****

Arthur wrapped his arms around a tree. He could only reach halfway around the powerful trunk. An ant crawled across his face and tickled his nose. His nostrils twitched. Arthur laughed. "Hi," he said to the ant. "I'm Arthur."

****

Cell four was in the back corner of Paxton prison. The air in the hallway was oddly still and serene as Sheila slowly approached the cell. Through the bars, she saw two lifeless bodies lying side-by-side on the floor.

****

You never know what ideas are roaming around in your head until you unlock the gates and set the animals free.

****

Karl looked at the trees in the field. They were beautiful as they were. But it was not enough.

He made them dance.

****

Music makes the trees come alive. And when trees come alive, they overwhelm and intimidate. When trees come alive, they make us feel like tiny specks of dust. When trees come alive, we finally see that we are nothing more than fools living in a brilliant universe.

APPENDIX

Achoophobia: (at-choo-faux-bee-ah) the fear of sneezing.

Gerald and Cheryl McQueen's 15 sons (in alphabetical order):
Adam McQueen
Andy McQueen
Basil McQueen
Braden McQueen
Dick McQueen
Fergus McQueen
Franklin McQueen
Hank McQueen
Harry McQueen
Jeremiah McQueen
Joffrey McQueen
Kirk McQueen
Mohammed McQueen
Preston McQueen
Walter McQueen

Gerald and Cheryl McQueen's 15 sons (in order of age, from eldest to youngest):
Dick McQueen
Basil McQueen
Joffrey McQueen
Harry McQueen
Jeremiah McQueen
Preston McQueen
Franklin McQueen
Andy McQueen
Braden McQueen
Mohammed McQueen

Adam McQueen
Walter McQueen
Hank McQueen
Kirk McQueen
Fergus McQueen

Gerald and Cheryl McQueen's 15 sons
(according to hair colour):
<u>BROWN</u>
Adam McQueen
Andy McQueen
Braden McQueen
Dick McQueen
Franklin McQueen
Harry McQueen
Jeremiah McQueen
Joffrey McQueen
Kirk McQueen
Mohammed McQueen
Preston McQueen

BLONDE
Basil McQueen
Fergus McQueen
Hank McQueen

BALD
Walter McQueen

Autodysomophobia: (awe-toe-diss-ohm-oh-faux-bee-ah) the fear of smelling terrible.

Autostultophobia: (awe-toe-stult-oh-faux-bee-ah) the fear of being stupid.

Permanium: see *parvalium*

Parvalium: see *permanium*

*Famous Classical Composers Who Died Before Age 60:

Classical Composer:	Age of Death:
Goldberg	29
Schubert	31
Bellini	33
Mozart	35
Bizet	36
Gershwin	38
Chopin	39
Weber	39
Scriabin	43
Strauss	45
Schumann	46
Mahler	50
Vranicky	51
Pachelbel	52
Borodin	53
Tchaikovsky	53
Debussy	55
Nietzsche	55
Beethoven	56
Satie	59

(*there are many, many lesser known classical composers who also died young)

Compsognathus: (komp-sawg-nayth-us) a small, bipedal, carnivorous dinosaur about the size of a turkey.